The Other Side of This

A Raver's Story Based on real life hallucinations

Written by

Jeffrey D Hubbard

The Other Side of This

A Raver's Story Based on real life hallucinations

Written by Jeffrey D Hubbard

Copyright 2013

DH Geoffries Publishing LTD

Malibu,CA

PH#1-323-804-2624

ISBN: 978-0-578-11011-0

Library of Congress Copyright 2009 #1-297824861

Writers Guild of America registered 2009 #1399714

3

Acknowledgements

Thank you first and foremost to the creator of the known and unknown universe. Without your guidance and loving hand I would have not been alive to tell the tale. Thank you to Terrance Mckenna,Timothy Leary, Albert Hoffman, Ram Dass, Aleister Crowley, Space Time Continuum, 1.8.7(Jordana), Stickman, Exploding Boy, Mary(Thank you for the blanket!), Ryan Matthew, Smartee, Sho, Dieselboy, UPS (Underground Peace Society), Yabette, Dj Natas, Christine, Eric the Red, Dj Keoki, Christiane , Hardfloor, Prototype 909,Derrick May, Majesty Events, Ed Luna, Doug Holmes, Collective Intelligence, Seek, Jordan, Vibeonauts, Planet Djax, Deelite, Lady Miss Kier, On-e, Shane ,Mike, Jill, Richie, T-Bone, Ant C, Troy, Todd W, Mr and Mrs Fernandez-Stuart, Marilyn Martin. Deepest thanks to my brother Steve who without his constant support, this book would have never seen the light of day. To my mother and father(R.I.P) for always loving me no matter what. To all the kids on the dance floors of planet earth and beyond, You are not alone. They can make laws against us, they can beat us down, they can run us out, they can try anything in their power and they will not stop our feet from moving to that underground beat. Lastly eternal thanks to TLV, you are my love and you will always be in my heart. And to everyone of the underground. This one is for you all. Keep smiles on your faces and your eyes to the sky. Freedom. Love. Unity. Independance. Delight.

Dedicated to the Ravers of the universe. Ravers Unite.

TABLE OF CONTENTS

Chapter 1

Tunnel Vision

The rain was pouring down in sheets. "I think we are going to die" explains Tim. "It's a great night to die" I answer with a steely grin.

The rain is washing out our brakes and we are hydroplaning down the highway into downtown Pittsburg, Pa. We were on our way to a rave in an underground tunnel. My brother and his girlfriend are leading the way in a separate car in front of us. Her brakes were obviously working because she was now quickly moving out of sight.

"Shit, she has the directions" slides Tim as she becomes a smear in the distance.

"We are fully screwed" I jolt back lighting up the skunky spliff.

The waves of green smoke fill the car as we careen down the highway. "Alien Dreamtime" pulses in the background with Terrance Mckenna's tryptamine voice slips out of the speakers into our fully lubricated minds. What to do now. We are sliding down a freeway into an unknown city with no map and no way of knowing where to begin to find directions. It's the only way to travel.

"Hey Jay, isn't DJ Exxon playing at the after party" Tim starts in with glee.

"There is a Exxon station over there" I belch out between drags. "Maybe we are supposed to go there to find directions to the tunnel".

Tim has a tripped out sensibility, we all kind of do I guess. Our merry band of rebels has lets say some "experience" with altered states of consciousness. The Exxon hint is a enough to make us head over to the gas station. Low and behold there is my brother and his wife sitting by the pay phone waiting for us like it was planned from the beginning.

"You guys ready for this" whips my brother with a leary smile.

All together there are two cars comprised of 7 people. Me ,Tim, My brother and the race car driver, and 3 other buddies from high school. Of the 7 only 3 of us had ever been to an underground party before. Steve, his girl and I. We had been going to raves for a few months when we heard about this legendary party that was going down in an freeway tunnel in Pittsburgh. Apparently the promoters had a pass from the mayor to film a "movie" in the tunnel. All who showed at the event were "extras". They acquired the permits to shut the tunnel down all night long. They were calling it "Tunnel Vision". The prospect of this type of party was mythical to us. We had been in some cool venues but this one was going to top them all.

We arrived at a parking lot covered in a mass of swirling colors and wide smiling faces. A girl had set up in the back of an old station wagon and was selling off tickets to the party. She was lit up like a pixy, tingling with energy. After buying up the tickets its off to the shuttle buses. We jump into the pristine white bubble buses an head up a hill. The bus is brimming with madness. People jumping over seats, laughing, playing. The bus stops at the top of a hill and dumps the mutants into the street. The party hasn't fully started yet, so all the lights are still on in the tunnel. The tunnel itself is called the Corlis Tunnel.

It was a two lane wide 250 yd half spherical tunnel that runs slightly down hill ending into a river on the other side of a two lane highway. The promoters have sectioned off both ends with giant tarps. At one end of the tunnel is a giant pyramid of tv screens with the dj set up at the top of the pyramid. A huge argon laser is set up behind the dj and shines on the tarp at the other end of the tunnel.

People are running around all over the place hugging, smiling, and scoring. We were on the hunt for LSD, acid, blotter, L, Lucy, paper, liquid, little ones, angel scrolls, whatever you wanted to call it. We had already pre-rolled a half once of prime skunk on the way and had another half saved back for the after party. We were all wearing post hippie wanna be pre raver clothing. Baggy jeans, Tie dyed shirts, big Dr Suess hats, laced with glow everything, strobes the whole nine.

My twin brother spots a local paper cat from a few weeks back. A little guy that beams with vibe. He has the fuel we need. The hits are huge. They call them Naked Ladies. They have little pictures of nubile beauties exposing their naked breasts. The acid is so thickly crystallized, the paper does not tear. It snaps. I buy 20 and my brother buys 10. Him and his girl take 5 each. Tim takes five and drops them in the gutter. Picks them right back up and chomps down. I take ten. Now this doesn't seem like that much in all reality but the smear is the hits were actually four to each picture. So my brother actually took 20. And I just took 40. Tim looks shocked.

"What the hell are you doing man, you don't need that

much" he says with a growing terror in his eyes.

"Oh calm down I just dropped 14 a few weeks back in a field, everything was cool just relax".

Not knowing I had just signed on for much, much more than I could have ever imagined.

See, I overlooked one of the most important "rules" ,if you will, of tripping. Setting. A field of flowers is a lot different than a underground tunnel with 2,000 maniacs dancing to the most advanced music on the planet. All synced up to a huge glowing alien pyramid from mars. Kind of like comparing Millbrook to Manhattan. They are clearing the tunnel for the party to begin.

We move slowly out of the tunnel as the acid starts to creep along with our little tribe of pranksters. It always starts so gentle. Innocent. Slipping up your spine. Your world ever so slowly transforming into a glowing ball of goo. You'll never see it coming. We finally stop at the top of the hill and begin to start our descent back down into the tunnel. The lights are off now and the tunnel is on full blast. Pounding bass surges up the hill while we slowly file into the laser green chasm. I turn on my industrial strength strobe light, playing with its light blasts on the surrounding crowds. The flash freezes everything. Its like watching a film in slow motion. A little raver next to me finds the strobe a bit much at the moment. I cease blasting the cosmic beams and slowly follow the leader into the rabbit hole below.

The only way I could describe the scene before me would be picturesque chaos. Pulsating bodies swarmed inside the booming chamber.

A huge laser beam placed behind the Dj's head is shining sacred geometric symbols on the rear end of the tunnel. Everyone was dancing. And I don't mean the two step or the fox trot. I am talking about dancing like there is no tomorrow. Really No tomorrow. Only the now. Pouring it out on the dance floor now. Pushing it. Feeling it. Sweating like this was the last party the earth was going to see. I get swallowed by the mass and immediately lose everyone. I am now swimming in a sea of demonic faces. Horns, glowing blood red eyes, dripping, giggling, warped faces. Sinister, fang laced grins from the depths of darkness. Everywhere I look melting piles of sloth filling my whole optical region. Holy shit. I am in hell. Panic . Fear . Escape. I begin swimming through the horde toward the exit. Everywhere the world melts into chaos. Heads with no bodies. Dis remembered souls wrenching all over the place. Get out. Almost there. I can see the exit. I am out of here. Its only been an hour. I think. What time is it? Where am I? What's going on?

  I find my way over to a curb right outside the tunnel opening. I sit down and try to collect myself. Not a chance. Everything is unattached. Layers of gooey color swirl in every direction as the acid takes a firm hold on my mind. The sky is swirling in ultraviolet pulses. The stars fall to the ground in firework streaks exploding on impact. The bushes behind me are starting to rustle and sway.

They start to grow and wrap down the pavement heading right for me. Just as I think I am about to be swallowed by the man eating bush, a person or something comes running out of the bushes flying past me, up the side of the hill that runs up over the tunnel.

I am going over the edge. There is nothing to hold onto. Disintegrating, melting, shifting, morphing ,swaying. A tall blonde man suddenly appears to my left. He is dressed in normal looking attire but was bending over asking me if I was ok. What do you mean ok. I am about to be eaten by a bush. No everything is not ok. I rapidly realize I was balling like a child and didn't even know it.

"You alright man, you looked pretty bad, you going to be ok" asks the tall stranger.

"Are you God" I whimpered back to him. "No, but I just spoke with him last night" he replied.

Holy shit. That's it. The tears started pouring. He is talking with god. Or is he god playing tricks on me because he cant let on his identity to a mere human. This stranger, later to be known as stickman, tried to console me but I had gone totally mad. I began whimpering to him.

"I need a mate, I need someone, I need a mate" over and over through the tears.

He left and came back with a beautiful blonde haired goddess named Samantha. She had huge blue eyes that you fell into. She radiated a beautiful pink glow.

"Its Ok." she purred into my ear. " Its just a party, you will be just fine.

Just come on back inside." "Its hell" I cried sheepishly.

"Its what you make it out to be, lets go back inside, you will be just fine."

I took a deep look inside. I could stay out here.

Run from my fears. Go home. Sleep it off. Sober up. None of that.

I am here and I need to face it. Face that fear deep inside and leap headlong into the unknown. There was no going back. She grabbed my hand as we descended into the swirling demon party below. No going back. I found my brother near the entrance of the tunnel. I abruptly asked,

"Are you god" "Stop pulling on me, you will be alright" he sternly replied .

I hadn't noticed I was trying to climb into his back pack. He was holding onto his last wits as much as I was. I needed to let go. Let go of the comfort. Face the darkness alone. I let go of his back and made my way to the very far back end of the tunnel. There were no people in the pitch darkness and only the huge rotating geometric symbols were visible. I laid down on the curb and shut my eyes. I figured I could sleep off the drug. Just take a little nap and it would be over. I didn't know it had only been two hours and this was merely the beginning. Wishful thinking at best. I began to project myself out of the tunnel. Drifting slowly into the darkness of my mind. I suddenly became aware of a grass field coming into focus. I began drifting closer and closer to this beautiful field on the edge of a gigantic forest. I have no idea where or why there was a huge Victorian style bed placed in the center of this field. I was floating toward this "bed" but when I say "I", "I" was not a body at this point. It was gone. I was out of body. I lay down upon this bed with a feeling of every lasting peace and love washing over me. Real peace. Real rest. Lying in this field time seemed to melt away in the distance.

I felt my "head and body on the bed but it was not visible. Left over resonance shadows of body living. Then with a sudden flash of blinding light.

"Hey, you cant sleep yet, the party has just begun" beams a little elfin type man with a red pointed beard.

This cosmic helper flashed his guidance beam on my eyes one more time for good measure and when I stood up the world as I once knew it was totally gone. I was standing in total darkness.

A voice or voices began speaking to me. I couldn't make out where it was coming from or why it was speaking to me. It whispered into my mind.

"You don't need the restriction of this world, let go" the voice shimmered.

I had meditated a few times before, High and sober. There is legend of the "voice" which speaks to one from another place. This voice would speak to an initiate to guide them through their right of passage. To be reborn from the constraints of the illusion of this world. To release the human soul into the cosmic soul of the unbound universe.

"You don't need those anymore" stated the motherly voice.

With almost unconscious impulse I had come to the conclusion that I needed to remove my clothing. I pulled off my shirt and folded it up. I took off my socks and shoes. Pants. And then my underwear. Free. Free from the world of constrained living. Naked to the world. Next I remember starting to dance. Dancing for the world.

Dancing for the salvation of my soul. Feeling every muscle moving in harmonious rhythm. The godhead pouring into every cell of my body cleansing my torn soul to the very core. I looked down noticing the floor starting to shimmer a effervescent watery purple gold. The material moved up along the walls creating huge stone like proto Egyptian type statues. The surface of these statues was not static but constantly changing in form and measure The surfaces kept changing as fast as I could look. Language systems, maps, archaic numbers, and strange faces all making up the skin. They kept growing larger and larger. Now they form the walls of a massive cavern. These figures grew to the height of at least 20 feet forming columns that went off into infinite distance. Their heads made up most of their body, which is covered in thousands of kaleidoscope eyes.

They were something totally alien from anything I had ever witnessed. A bright light shown off in the distance with the alien statues forming the walls of this massive grotto. The light was very small and very far away. Even at this distance I could feel its rays of love shining into my soul. And now a sea of demonic faces stands between me and this bright loving light. Legions of old waiting to rip my soul apart piece by piece if I show any fear or hesitation. The tunnel began to slop steeper and steeper. It is now as if I was at the bottom of a pit and this light was growing farther and farther away. I started to dance through the sea of despair. These demons had many faces. The cackling of envy. The grown of sloth. The screech and whine of vanity. I began to notice the demons were reflections of me. Things inside me. Thing that existed inside of everyone. These were not external demons created by some evil force. These were the dark choices everyone must battle our their path of life. Things I could be. Things that I would do. Sins that would become. or not. That these demons were not separate from me. They were me.

The ground beneath my feet began dissolving into a watery blue liquid. I danced harder and harder. It felt like I was dancing out of my skin. Releasing all the weight of my life. Letting go completely. Fully. I looked in front of me and now the demons were gone. Now a vast ocean lay before my eyes. I picked up speed and jumped headlong into the warm ocean waters that lay before me. In reality I had dove face first into the pavement. I was swimming in the ocean now moving effortlessly through the blue velvet liquid. I noticed a pack of rainbow colored dolphins swimming next to me. They smiled with warmth, as I started to notice something very peculiar. My body was gone now and I was now a dolphin too.

I was one of their tribe. The feeling of connection to my brother and sister species was overwhelming to say the least. There was a feeling of pure freedom. Slipping and sliding along the ocean blue. A true paradise. I felt home for the first time in my life.

While I was swimming with the pod I noticed we were getting closer to the bright shinning light. It pulled me. It called to my spirit. It was home. That was where we were headed. I found myself dancing again in my pseudo "human" form. I started dancing harder and harder moving faster closer. I was leaving my skin behind. Going into the light. Nothing can stop me. The bright shining light that I was heading for was the visual screens at the front of the event. It looked like a gleaming shining pyramid doorway into another planet. Suddenly a feel hands grabbing me from all directions. The demons. The demons were trying to stop me from paradise. In reality it was some concerned fellows trying to stop me from running through the center of the stage. Now I am struggling with huge demons that are pulling my body limb from limb. They grab my arm but I mentally drop the arm as I slip through their grips. I dive over some vending booths giving chase to the hordes. They grab hold this time with a firm grip. With one last fling I slip my body lose from their hands and fly headlong into the tunnel wall smacking my head firmly against the concrete. This has got to be one of the strangest sensations that I have ever experienced. It felt as if the wall was made of paper and as I hit my head I just passed right through it. And I just kept going. Now totally freed from my body. I found myself in what I would call a light body. I looked like a shimmering blue and purple stream of semi solid translucent crystal. I was now shooting up a gigantic gem laced tunnel or chasm of some sort.

I noticed there were other beams of light traveling next to me. These beams of light start to communicate with me.

"What do you want to be" giggled one of the beams radiating pinks and oranges.

" You can go anywhere, be anything you want, anything you can think, anything you can dream, its all possible"

"What does it feel like to be a woman?" I unconsciously ask to the beings.

My "body" was immediately thrust into a pleasure grip

beyond on all heights of the human imagination. The light beings begin laughing with glee.

"That was a woman's orgasm!!!!"

As all this is going on in my "head", my physical body was left unconscious. People began pouring gutter water on me , and then started giving it to me to drink. Then they began pouring it all over my body. It felt like the descriptions I hear about baptisms. Feeling all my guilt and pain and suffering being washed out of my body. The warm fluid feeling of love taking the place of fear and pain. A rebirth into the underground of the human mind. The places no human dared dwell from fear of never finding their way back. After this rapid influx of sensory input had subsided , I began to feel more comfortable in my new "body of light". I noticed the light beings were guiding me towards a vast city of flowing rainbow glass. And as soon as I lay my eyes upon the city I was in it. A city of such wonder it pains me to write about it. The curved shaped buildings molded and flowed into one another with perfect rhythm. I walked along huge streets of liquefied gold rolling like a bubbling stream at play. In this kingdom there was no restriction of anything. No gravity. No skin. No boundaries. No pain. No suffering. Whatever you dreamt was a reality. There was a connected aspect to everything that surrounded me. Your spirit was connected to every other molecule that ever existed. It felt as if I was being giving a tour of a grand new world and it was created for me. A new born baby walking into a new world for the first time.

Back in real time my body had died. A nurse was summoned to check my vitals before an ambulance was called. No pulse. Panic was setting in. The decision needed to be made quickly to save my life.

Back in my head or out of my head depending on your point of view, I was being led out of the city of glass.

I was now perched on a huge grassy knoll with rolling hills as far as the eyes could see. My body is different now. Its getting solid. I can feel the weight of gravity like an old hand reaching from a cold dark grave. I can sense someone next to me. It has a female presence to it.

"You are not over sex yet, you have to go back" it seethed into my ear, almost with a dark hint of humor.

As this entity spoke these words into my ear the world began to grow darker and darker. The world of light had passed before my eyes in just a glimpse of time.

"We have a pulse, his pulse is back" as the nurse scrambled to control me.

When I woke up I immediately tried to jump up and run for it. She held me down without much trouble once she was sitting on top of me.

"Get him out of here" demanded the very worried promoter. Its not good business to have someone die at your party. Things get a bit fuzzy from here. I remember flashing back and forth between the ultra paradise heaven world and "This". I was moved onto the same little shuttle buses that had taken us up the hill at the beginning of the party. It ripped down the hill and arrived at Steve's car with lighting speed. I was now in his back seat and we are flying down the Pittsburgh highway. Steve and Tracy had both transformed into light beings driving me through the liquid city. Then flash back to dark third world reality with skin and bones. Every time I would find myself in this world I would begin weeping uncontrollably. Praying to the almighty lord of lords to take me back paradise. Steve had been very scared up to this point about me really dieing. They lost my pulse once and he didn't want it to happen again. So he had decided to make a go for the hospital. Mind you he is on half of what I took and is now driving through the city higher than the rooftops. As he pulled into the hospital all hell broke loose. Blinking lights, screaming sirens and police. Police everywhere.

"Fuck this" my brother announces "there is no way we are going in there". He makes a quick u turn sweeping the car around for an abrupt about face.

I began to lose consciousnesses. Steve just hit the gas and drove. He had no idea where but to just drive out of the city and hope for the best. As we moved into what seemed to be dew covered foothills, Steve noticed we were no longer on the ground. I looked out the window and saw the tops of the telephone poles as we drifted into the night sky. And then suddenly just as in so many ufo folklore legends, we were sitting in a dunkin doughnuts 30 miles from the city. The sun was already firmly fixed in the sky (we left the event at 2am which means 4 hours had passed but no one in the car can remember what the hell happened.) and we were stuck on earth in a major way.

The drug was still very evident in my optical range but no mind power on earth could take me back to the world of paradise and light. The feeling of homesick cant even begin to scratch the surface of what was now weighing down on me. Being locked up back in this skin suit to do time as a "human". To have felt freedom for only a fleeting second to be bound up in gravitational skin prison once again.

This was a comedown to rival all other come downs in history.

I made it home past my mom (I was going to university fulltime, working fulltime, and living at home) and headed straight for the shower. I girl named Mary had giving me a blanket to cover me up at the tunnel, so I had at least something to cover me up from the car to the house. Once in the bathroom I got to finally see the damage I had brought upon myself. I was covered head to toe in black grimy sludge slim. No skin was visible the through the curtain of grim. I had scratches from head to toe from my Olympic try out dive into the pavement but beyond that nothing else was damaged but my mind. I didn't know where I was. What planet I was on. Why people kept calling me by these names that I did not know. It felt like I was in a dream world and that I would be waking up from it anytime. That I would just wake up back in paradise. That this couldn't be real. Family affair is next week. I should be able to leave this planet far behind and make my way back to my home planet. Just a few days and I will be back. This cant be it.

Chapter 2

Cosmic Runway

It's the Friday after my trip down the tunnel and we are headed to Family Affair. This is an outdoor event held in north eastern Ohio produced by the UPS crew(underground peace society).We are heading up on Thursday and staying at the coffee house which is hosting a little pre-party. Our tribe for this journey consists of steve, tracy and myself. Pointless to say after last week, we have very high hopes for a great time (even though most people would be done with such things after ripping their clothes off and diving into pavement in front of 2,200 people).The pre party is in full swing when we arrive. The crowd is small and very intimate. Yabette of UPS is playing some live ambient grooves. There are some low key visuals swirling over simple mood lighting. The atmosphere is quite chill and everyone seems in good spirits. We hang around till the end of the show taking every second that we could in. The owner George said we could stay the night if we wanted to. He had extra couches that he didn't mind lending to weary travelers like ourselves. This kind of open mentality was very common in the early days of the Midwest scene. It was a mixture of Midwest values crossed over with DeadHead ethics dipped in the beginnings of the computer boom. We all wanted a place of freedom. We had heard of freedom in books and movies. We had never really got to experience "freedom" for lack of a better term. We lived in a area of the country that had a literal stranglehold on the minds that grew up here. To think, act or be different from the herd was frowned on and set to those "peace freaks" on the coasts.

We just wanted a place to be ourselves. To explore our imaginations that we had lost in our childhood past. Even if that meant only one night out of the week.

At least that day was ours. We awoke feeling the excitement of the day sparkling throughout the coffee house. We head out to the venue which is about 1 hour into the forest. The roads wind to and fro pushing deep into groves of beautiful oak trees. The air is humming with insect song stretched out on the mid summers breeze. Eventually we arrive at Beavercreek campgrounds with day glow freaks beginning to show up from every direction. We are vending little no nothings like little bottles of bubbles and glow sticks which allows us to get in with some discounts. We drive up the dirt road past the various campsites being set up next to the main stage. We go left into what looks like a small race track which has high bent rusted fences hanging around the circle. This is the designated vending area and our home base for this evenings launch . Steve pulls out our tables while Traci sets out the bubbles. There is another crew setting up next to us representing the MASSIVE magazine collective from Milwaukee. The group of five young males is pounding hardcore with utter abandon, twirling all around like mad dervishes. They were firing off fireworks in every direction screaming with laughter at every blast. Hooting, laughing, screeching, giggling, crying like some pack of mutated raving animals. This crew's party didn't start or stop. They were a party.

"We have been up for 3 days on caffeine pills and its getting really fun",one of them explains as his huge smile blinds us from seeing the fireworks being thrown over our heads.

Time for me to get out my half of skunk and smoke the hell down. The sun is blazing down on us out on the dirt race track as we sit for what seems like hours. When your waiting for the sun to go down it can take a long time. I rolled up a nice huge joint and lit the green essence. Ahh seems to make everything get a little better. The sun starts to feel so wonderful, time starts to begin to feel full and makes every second a gift instead of a curse. Time to go and search out lucy (LSD) for the nights events.

This mission is left up to me, Steve and Tracy will hold down the bubble fort. I start wandering down through the festival grounds when I come upon a dorky looking fellow. He was wearing a dead shirt with some shorts that didn't match. In fact he really looked like he was going to an event for the first time.

"Hey man looking for some paper" he says to me in a low innocent voice.

At a distance I thought he might be a younger teenager but on closer inspection he is actually much older. His was hiding this fact underneath his beat up fisherman hat. I snatched up what he had and went off a very happy camper. I made my way back to the glow shop to find steve and tracy frying in the afternoon sun.

" I got everything we need for tonight" I explain with a shit eating grin of an acid beam.

They both flash back approving smiles. We are starting to get very excited for tonight's lift off. I sit back down to roll a celebratory spliff (potheads don't need much of an excuse to celebrate with the scared herb) as a hipped out raver dressed in black is making his way over.

"Hey anyone looking for some greens" whipping out a fresh once of beautiful lime green sacrament.

"Nope got my own man but I do have some DMT I made a few days back" I shoot back.

Now a little history on this particular DMT extraction that was being offered by yours truly. DMT is a highly hallucinatory chemical that exists in thousands of plants and animals including humans. In humans it comes into reaction in the neural pathways of the brain at the point of physical death. This chemical is the chemical that lets your mind know your body is about to die and its time for the soul to leave. The extraction I had made had come from a phallaris grass plant that I had grown in my mom's back yard. Through certain methods(a wheatgrass juicer and some grain alcohol) you can extract this chemical out of the grass and smoke it upon drying. When you smoke DMT you are tricking your mind into thinking the dying state is happening. So you basically are inducing a trial death. The big mistake is that I did not try out the extraction on myself before the show to make sure everything was ok. A very big dumb amateur mistake. So my new skunk buddy wanted 2 grams of course.

The sun is beginning its descent and its time to drop Ms. Lucy. My bro and Tracie drop 4 and I drop 8.I figure my tolerance is up pretty high. As the darkness settles in the acid starts kicking in. Everything is starting to get electric as someone comes out of the shadows.

"That shit was bunk" explained the voice.

It wasn't the guy i had dealt with before.

This slickly dressed guy looked very similar to Mr. deadhead newbie I had got the paper from earlier.

"Man I made that shit myself" with the shivering feeling of wondering if I had fucked up the extraction. Maybe it was bunk.

"Come on man let's go try it out" exclaims my new buddy with the tone that made me feel I didn't have a choice ,even if I thought I did.

"Ill be right back Steve, I'm going to go and deal with this" looking back at my now very worried brother.

I guess wandering off in the dark with a drug dealer you just supposedly sold bunk drugs to would probably make most sane people very fucking nervous. We start walking to the back of the festival grounds toward a huge hill that goes straight up forming a kind of wall that the main stage was pointing towards. As we are slowly trekking up the slope, it begins to get steeper and steeper. From out of the corner of my eye I noticed to little figures moving towards our general direction. They appear to be two very small candy dressed female ravers. They our now directly in our path and start to walk besides me as we stagger up the hill.

"You really scared us last week, please don't do that again" says one of them in a very stern voice for such a little creature.

"I don't plan on it, but it wasn't all that bad", feeling highly embarrassed these two girls had seen me naked as a judge.

"Dying is a very serious matter, its not a joke".

"Please do be careful" explains the other little one as they disappear down the hill slope into nothing.

"This looks like a good spot" explains "the dealer". We are half way up the steep hill on a little position over looking the party. I sit down and my guest strolls over to some other travelers to our right. He returns with a huge 3 foot long glass pipe.

"This will work for the DMT right?" he smirks as my jaw gravitates in disbelief.

He hands me back the DMT I had sold his buddy and I hand back the 25 dollars. The dealer whips out a huge roll of cash and laughs at my money.

"We just lost a 35,000 dollar purple laser but its ok. Things will work out."

I unwrap the foil package containing the DMT. Its a chunky black tar substance that smells of rotted grass stains. I am really starting to get worried if its going to work or not. The acid is really ripping through my mind with waves of intense paranoia. This guy obviously didn't care about the 25 bucks ,so why the fuck all this. So I did the most logical thing and packed all the DMT that was there(enough for 10 doses at least). I started to smoke the huge interstellar chalice with long drags of the harsh thick smoke. I passed to my buddy and he pulled hard as well. Pass. Hit. Pass. Hit. After 4 or five exchanges the dealer poses a very unique question.

"Have you ever felt dimensions folding on top of dimensions" he slightly wisps.

My new companion begins to shape shift into what

appeared to be a hyper dimensional shimmering space elf shaman. His face and jaw widened and stretched. His pupils swelled beyond the limits of his eyes. His nose flattened and his ears grew to double the original length. His legs molded into the earth around him while his whole body began to hum from every direction. Then within a blink of an eye he was back to his human form pulling on my arm.

"Hey man let's go to the top" pointing to the top of what now appeared to be a shear dirt mountain slope rising straight into the starry night sky.

Closing near the top of the slope it gets so steep I am scrambling on my hands and knees praying I am going to make it up this dam thing. Not to mention I just smoked a massive amount of DMT and dropped 8 hits of acid an hour ago. Now I'm climbing mount trip a lot with a shamanic dream traveler. I finally manage to the top and there are two other individuals waiting for us. I crouch on the edge of the cliff with the other 3 "humans" and gaze out over the site laid before me. The party is out below us in full blazing glory. The sound is roaring up the cliff face filling up every cell in my body with magnetic ecstasy. The event appears as a huge kaleidoscope heart that is pumping humans in and out of its massive organic arteries to the rhythm of the funkiest alien language in this part of the known universe. The spirit of our mother planet pulsating through every one of our sweet souls. I begin to notice what looks like multi colored spinning spiral space craft slowly descending out of the sky into the area of the event. The crafts were in all different shapes and sizes and colors.

They were slowly descending from all directions and right before landing they would transform into normal looking cars.

I notice what looks like huge beams of light guiding the spacecraft into the event safely. A kind of cosmic traffic guide coming from the sky behind me. I followed the beams (the stage was way in front of me) and looked up at something beyond the reaches of my mind. 4 15-20 foot tall pure white "alien beings" where standing behind us. Each one was holding a huge light beam emitter of some sort. These "emitters" were projecting these huge beams down on the party and into the sky above. These beams seemed some how to connect to the stage beams to form some type of hyper dimensional guidance system that directs traffic to the event.

"Holy fuck bro I think I'm losing it" I whimper to my new found drug dealing space shaman.

One of the others chimes in.

"Its ok your going to be just fine, have you ever used your voice before?"

"Use my voice?" I query back as I can feel my mind losing its grasp on reality as a whole.

The voice is of a girl. A very smooth almost hypnotic voice. She begins to hum a mid range "aum" which shudders directly through my body. One of the other shadows starts in with a bass tone.

"You can do this to, its easy, try" as a tone begins to come from my mouth almost subconsciously.

The other is now forming a very shrill treble tone while my

tone grows louder to match the middle tone of the girl. Now all four of us are humming. Now all our "voices" are forming one harmonious tone. The perfect tone, unified through 4 human voices focused together in one sound. I begin to notice my whole body shaking. The "tone" reaches deafening proportions as a beam of clear light erupts from my mouth. I feel some type of energy beam from above pulling me off the earth. I grab hold of the cliff in total shock, as my body falls gently back down to the ground. The light beam disappears from my mouth and I start to come out of whatever I was just in.

"Hey aren't you the naked guy from tunnel vision" shouts the girl who just taught me how to use my voice as a spaceship. She jumps across the others tackling me with a huge hug.

"We are so happy your ok ,we didn't think you were going to ever be the same, let alone be here now, up here with us".

I notice a large neon colored figure making its way through the crowd below. Its getting larger coming toward the base of the hill.

"Hey, is that you up there Jay" bellows the neon striped creature. "Steve, is that you".

"Yea its me where the fuck have you been?" which is a pretty good question, being his brother just disappeared two hours ago on a head full of acid with a pissed off drug dealer. I'll have to explain the space traveling elf story for later.

I say my goodbyes to my new found space friends and slowly slide down the dirt slope with my brothers worried, disapproved face getting closer into focus.

"Where in the world did you disappear to".

" If you only knew, if you only knew".

I am now at the bottom of the dirt slope and smack dab in the middle of an alien freak out love fest. There is a basic stage with a dj set up and huge stacks of speakers on both sides of the stage. The dance floor is sand and the dancers have taking big pieces of card board to use as dancing platforms. This was the first time I truly witnessed the extent of "liquid breaking". They look as if their bodies are breaking into pieces with the smooth artistry of a robotic ballet dancer. One dancer looks like he broke off his arm at the shoulder, then reattached it around his back. Another one has knees that flip ,flop and fold slowly melting into the dance floor below. Flowing, fluid creative bodies all moving in perfect harmonious rhythm with each other.

The main floor was surrounded by vans and vendors of all shapes and sizes. One particular van has a huge projection screen put behind it. It is laid out against the hill and they are playing video games. The very familiar hiss of a nos tank is coming from the vicinity. Come to find out these jolly fellows were emitting nitrous oxide into the dance floor area. So if you stood in the right spot at the right time you would be standing directly in the nos stream and flying to planet rave on the wings of mind numbing pleasure. The music was funky and thunderous. You could see the atmospheric haze of human sweat created by the dance floor ritual. The party was at its "peak" as they say. When everything flows effortlessly. No separation between anyone in attendance.

A feeling of pure wholeness. Together as one.

Then the fires of hell burst forth from the deep.

At the front of the stage, one side of the speaker stacks burst into a huge ball of flames. The music screeches to a madding halt. Stage hands are running around with fire extinguishers like a scene out of apocalypse now. Total silence falls on the now dumb founded crowd. From this dead air comes a shimmer of life. A tiny crack in the abysmal silence. One person begins to clap. Another begins blowing their whistle in time with the clap. Then the rest of the crowd joins in this human band. A song begins to emerge louder than the sound system had ever been. A song created from the fires of chaos. A creation that reminded us that we are the music. The dj is us and we are the dj. The universal song of love and compassion will always be heard no matter if there is electricity or if a stack a speakers just blew up in front of your face.

And as the human song crescendos, the music kicked back on in full regale. Away the alien circus goes, as if nothing had skipped a beat. Truly a magical experience.

The night began to drag into the morning sun as the come down kicked in. The central nervous system can only handle so much input before it begins to fight against you. I flopped my drained body on a bench and began to roll the last of my skunk. Feeling very disillusioned about having not taking off back to my home world, a intense feeling of depression was setting in. What has just happened to me. I few weeks ago everything was fine in my world. and now I don't even know how I got on this planet or for that matter how to get the hell off it. George, the owner of the coffee house, swankers over as I'm puffing away into the depths of self pity.

"Hey you ever heard of Dubtribe before" he states with a smooth smile of self fulfillment.

"Nope, I never have" I respond with a mortified feeling of newbie ignorance.

"Here, puff on this. Let's walk over the hill and check them out" he answers back handing me a blunt of some of the sweetest smoke I had ever tasted. We walked over the little knoll behind the vending area where a van had set up speakers to each side of it. There was a small group of people dancing to music that moved my soul like never before. It was a slow, smooth, solid funk. It was like a message sent straight from my planet. It was medicine for my wounded mind. I laid back in the grassy field and soaked in the beats moving through my bones. My mind floats away on skunk induced clouds of neon cotton candy basslines. This world isn't so bad I guess. It does have its charm in some ways.

But these peculiarities could not begin to fill the void left by leaving my home world. After the nights events, one question remains firmly fixed into my mind. When can I get off this planet. When?

Chapter 3

New York Magik

The summer drifted on with a few more parties but no way off the planet whatsoever. We traveled to Iowa for a party named Ravestock. This was touted to be the rave equivalent of wood stock. What it turned out to be was a bunch of ravers in a corn field who had traveled long distances and paid 50 dollars a ticket to be there. Most left wondering where the hell the stages were. In true raver form we made the best of it. As it also turned out it was my brothers "bachelor party"(or a very weak attempt at) so it was kind of a bummer to say the least. No stages, no sound but from the cars, and we ate all our acid on the trip out here. Nothing to do but find the Nos tanks and forget where the hell we were. My brother had volunteered to go and pick up some djs at the airport so my buddy john and I were left to the campgrounds. We ran into some guys who were from Collville that I had met at family affair. There were two cute ass little girls with them and they were buying balloons by the fist full. My brother eventually returned having met some interesting people along the way including a promoter from Industrial strength records(who left his entire contact book in the back of our car and just happened to be from nyc, more on that later).We smoked and rolled our way through the event meeting freaks from everywhere along the way. The next morning my brother and our buddy had become aware they slept in a spider den(the tent hadn't been shut so there were literally hundreds of spiders crawling every where they had slept).We left the grounds sick, tired and broke. Sometimes you win, sometimes you lose.

A few weeks later, after my brother had walked down the aisle with his new wife Tracy(and a very embarrassing moment where I decided to threaten the dj to play a orbital song and danced like a crazed mad man in front of my family and friends), one of my friends called me up and said someone needed a riding partner to go to new york and pick up some sheets of acid. It was one of the girls that I had met a few weeks earlier at the Iowa corn field. I had been hanging out with the two girls since then and felt pretty excited to go to new york for the first time with a cute ass little raver chick. Her name was Tena. We were to meet up at taco bell to take off to the big apple. I met up with Tena and Todd, our buddy who was putting in money on the deal.

Tena's ride was a little late model Mazda which would be our ship into the great unknown. Tena was a little thing about 5 foot tall with reddish brown hair and freaky green/gray cat eyes. She had a very lean body and you could tell she had worked out extensively in her past. We spent most of our time on the way to new york caught in small talk most people end up in on a long road trip with someone you don't know. Tena had brought along a few ounces of dirty brown(it didn't matter, she was so cute it could have been mold) . I rolled up joints compulsively to break the tension of being very attracted to her. We talked a little background on where we were going and who we would be meeting. We were to be staying at her high school friend's apartment near the park on 109th I think. Her name was Christine. She was in new york trying to make it on Broadway as a singer. She also had the connection to the acid we were going to be getting our hands on. I had never been to new york before, so needless to say I was filled to the brim with excitement and complete fear. I had always heard of the madness of new york. The crime, the dirt, the killings, the whole media rap. but anything was better than sitting in Ohio another weekend doing the same domesticated primate dance.

Ever since I crashed landed on this very alien world that was supposed to be my home, I had a never ending feeling of not being in the right "place".I had walked off my job, dropped out of school, and was now on a drug run in a matter of weeks. Everything that had been ok a few weeks ago was now completely foreign to me. So a change in environment should be good right?

We pull into the big apple on a beautiful sunny afternoon and find the apartment with no effort. It was a large apartment building very near what looked to be central park. Walking up to the entrance I notice the gutters littered with little crack vials. I really hope this is a good idea.

We went up the stairs and were let in by Christine. The apartment is very small with one little room as a common area and a even smaller bedroom in the back. Classic new york living. Christine is a bubbly character(as most in the Broadway scene) about 5'4" with long brown hair and flaming brown eyes. She is very excited to see Tena, so I back off and let them catch up. Christine also has a boyfriend staying with her that is a joy to behold. This fellow is a self proclaimed devil worshipper that has sold his soul to the devil in order to be famous(fucking wonderful).This guy has built an altar in the bedroom with a dagger and the whole nine. Where the fuck am I and why the fuck did I think this was a good idea. Oh I almost forgot. The acid. Christine's friend was on his way ,so we chatted more fucking small talk waiting for the man to get here.

When the man did show up it was surely a sight to regard. His name was "Eric the red" or at least that's what we called him. He was a little guy about 5'5 with long red hair and a face which showed his age and lifestyle. He has very stressed eyes with a mouth that never really curves or shows any emotion at all. Turns out Eric only wants to sell books of acid(10 sheets) and we only have enough money for 4.Perfect. We just drove 8 hours to this god forsaken apartment to see a shit load of acid that we couldn't afford to get. fuck me big time. Phone calls need to be made. I know no one with any money (of course) so Tena starts calling her people. She gets a hold of her friends Jill and Richie and they get convinced to wire the money. Eric the red smiles ever so happily. We head out to find the local western union and try to get this money. Eric and Christine stay behind while Tena and I start wandering. We found a place pretty easy and got very weird looks. Two kids from Ohio getting 2500.00 dollars wire transferred to NYC. What, is this not proper behavior in the big city or what.

We walk back to the apartment with the greatest expectations. We were finally going to get the prize we oh so wanted in our minds. It is very hard to find lsd during these times, so picking up a legit connect is a big time deal. We get back to the apartment ready for business. Eric the red is very happy now that we have the money and begins to loosen up a bit. He pulls out a medium sized plastic baggy with sheets inside. he has decided to give us the "magic" sheets. The sheets have a black and white op art design with the word "magic" printed on it. Pretty serious looking stuff. He now only has five sheets and now we have to go get the rest from his buddy. Yes we were wet behind the ears to say the least folks. We also called up our little friend from ravestock (remember the lost contact book guy from industrial strength records) who's name happens to be Natas (reverse it).He is very thrilled to know we are in new york and have his contact book. He informs us he will be there immediately. While we are waiting for him to arrive, the red opens up a bit. I ask him if he has ever tried DMT. He gives me a quick unexpected stare before answering,

"Yea ,you get to talk to aliens".he has nothing more to say on the subject.

Why aren't there schools researching that we have a molecule in our grasp that can project us to alien worlds. Mind blowing. Natas has just arrived with much glee. he is a little guy 5'4" maybe with jet black hair and fashionable urban attire. he is very happy to see his little black book.

"You have saved my life, my whole life is in this book" he exclaims as he hugs his book.

"I'm going to show you guys around the city, give you the 2 dollar tour of the underground" he gleams.

I decide its a good idea to test out our goods before we head out to meet red's buddy and get our tour from natas.

"hey man, new york acid is a little stronger than what your probably used to, be gentle" natas warns with very worried look on his face.

"Ill be fine", I exclaim with young ignorance, plopping 3 hits on my tongue. The girls take 1 and Red takes out a personal sheet he has stashed away.

"This is Fly paper, some of the strongest acid around" he shoots ripping off a hit jamming it into his mouth.

Natas, Christine, Tena and myself get into Tena's car. Red gets into his. The acid is already starting to creep up my spine as we follow Red to our next destination. We turn right onto Broadway when all of a sudden all hell breaks loose. From ever direction NYPD cars surround our car with full sirens and lights. Holy fuck, that's it we are all going to jail. Its a set up. We all freeze like ice cubes. So many people think that when you get popped you can just eat your stash before they get you. Not this crew, we were frozen in complete fucking terror. We have 5 sheets of acid on us. Tena's driving tripping and we have a quarter pound of weed. We are all going to jail for a long time. Then as fast as they surrounded us they were gone. the streets are completely empty. Some how Red was still in front of us and we follow him to the side of the road. He gets out laughing like no other.

"Boy ,I bet you guys just shit yourself" with a glinting acid grim.

"The pope just went by, that was his escort "he whimpers still trying to control his hysterical laughter at our expense.

Man, I tell you I have never been that scared in my whole life. Now the acid was kicking in hardcore. Red goes around a corner to get the rest of what we are owed

,3 more sheets. he comes back very quickly(probably had it on him, just didn't want us to know) and hands us the rest of the goods.

"You guys be careful out here, ill see you soon" he waves as we get back on the road.

We have to stop in the village to meet up with Natas's girlfriend who has been calling him since we first met up with him.

"I just have to calm her down then we will go out on the town" he explains.

"I can drive to, so you guys can enjoy yourself" as Tena hands him the keys.

We head back down Broadway, going to the east village where ever that is. The acid has turned everything liquid on me and its only been an hour. Fuck maybe I shouldn't have taken so much.

"Turn around and look" explains Christine.

I turn around with my jaw hitting the floor in total awe. Time square lay before me in all its radiant glory. It looked like a huge alien spaceport rising into a massive gem filled sky. Gigantic billboards burst like neon firebombs exploding into millions of pixilated animations. Jell-O skyscrapers liquefy and soften into alien architecture I could have never dreamed of in my wildest Dalian fantasy. My mind was racing beyond any capacity it had measured before.

We stop at Natas's place for him to talk to his girl ,so we wait in the lobby of the building. Everything is dissolving and disintegrating in every direction I can try to focus on.

The tiles on the floor began growing out of the ground and turn into little muti colored columns of light. Tena's face keeps shifting and melting leading to even more panic since she is the only one that I know, and now she doesn't look like her any longer. Natas reappears with a very upset girlfriend in tow.

"I'm taking them out for their first time in new york, you'll get over it "he exclaims in a very smooth nonchalant voice.

She says nothing with a huff of breath and she's gone. We head out into the space station called New York. We begin walking to what is explained to me to be the "east village".The acid is now me and I am not. Everything in my view turns into a fantastical scene from one of Dante's sectors of hell. Transvestite, freaks, bums, gangsters, punks, hoods, any walk of life you can muster up in your darkest nightmares. People being led around with chains on their necks crawling on all fours with their master wearing a leather mask. and I'm not talking a few I'm talking about hordes of hellish creatures. I begin to feel my soul wanting to pull out of this situation, as I tell Tena my clothes are coming off. My clothes felt as if they were sliding off my body, but in actuality I was beginning another striptease tunnel vision style.

"You are not taking your clothes off" Tena states sternly as she grabs me by my arm and leads me off into central park.

Mind you its 1am in one of the most dangerous parks in the country(at the time) and two whitey idiots are heading off to the center of it with no idea where the fuck we were. We find a bench and I sit down. It feels like I'm melting through the steel. Creatures began coming out of the darkness peering into our little world. Spiked leather demons licking their chops waiting for the time to pounce.

"I cant take anymore, I want to go home, I want my mom" i dribble as the tears begin to flow.

"you cant go home ,we are in new york city and your going to have to deal with it " Tena slides back.

I lay my head down on her lap, searching for any comfort out here in this unknown forbidden territory. As soon as I lay my head down the whole world changes in a flash. The sun was now fully shining on me. The night had been removed and replaced with a beautiful summer day. Gorgeous birds flying around singing a divine songs of love.

 Flowers growing out of the ground in every direction you could see filling the air with heavenly aromatic bliss. Child like figures laughing and dancing over rolling emerald green fields. Then as fast as this world came, it went. We were slammed back into darkness. Back on this globe of suffering and pain. I began to regain control over the situation as we made our way back to natas and Christine. We walked past the now defunct "limelight" which was now boarded up like a crack house(the promoter, Michael alig, was being investigated for murder).

"Yea I was there when they raided it, they found someone dead in the bathroom" Natas states with certain uneasiness.

We get to the car with complete exhaustion setting in on my mind.

I rest myself on the wonderfully soft seat(we must have walked miles, because my body is wrecked) and start to come down on the way back to Christine's. Natas leaves us with sincere goodbyes(thank god he was with us, it could have gotten real bad) and we go up to Christine's little abode. Safety or at least I thought so.

We get upstairs and sit down to some joint rolling. Things seem to be winding down as Christine begins to talk very strangely.

"Its coming on in geometrics" she shakily states in a whimper.

This shouldn't be, we are all coming down. I took three times the amount they did, and I'm ready for bed.

"I just took 7 more hits a few minutes ago" Christine states as her face begins to shake in waves of seizure.

"You did what" i exclaim getting every fucking nervous.

I know what 3 hits just did to me. Christine said she had never done more than one hit in a sitting. And this is some of the best acid I have ever done. This can't be good.

"Well I cant let her go alone" says Tena as she reaches for the acid and drops seven herself.

Holy shit, now I have two girls I barley know on 8 hits of acid in a devil worshipers apartment. I take 4 more. when in Rome right? We are now all totally out our minds again. I just peaked hard a few hours ago, so I am not going to far, but the girls were on one big time.

Christine is going into fits of tears and laughter as Tena

begins stating " I can rewind my brain and fast forward it like a tape machine" with sweeping motions from her arms showing how it worked.

"chech cheh, rewind, hahahahhaha" she says over and over again.

"I can see a city, I cant go but I can peak in "she mumbles in a raving stampede.

I just sit there trying to keep calm and make sure no one did anything to nuts. and they were totally nuts. The sun is starting to come up and so is the boyfriend of Christine.

They disappear for a few seconds, before devil man storms out of the room towards me.

"Who the fuck do you think you are some acid guru or something 'he yells with veins coming out of his forehead.

"How dare you give her that much, she is out of her mind".

"Well first off I got this shit from HER and she did this on her own" i pierce back smoothly.

He thinks about yelling some more but decides leaving might be a better idea.

"Fuck you and your peace and love" ,as he slams the door. Man could this get anymore fucked up.

After devil man leaves we decide to take the party up to the rooftop. Both girls are absolutely out of it. Christine sits down on the roof and starts to weep uncontrollably. Her face starts to literally change form from the amount of energy flowing through her. She starts to look more and more like an alien transforming right in front of my face.

Man what the fuck do I do but try and calm them down.
the roof is your typical roof in Manhattan. It looks onto
nothing but more buildings. I can't tell if its raining or if its
grim coming from the city in the form of garbage smelling
mist. Tena is fully immersed in her own reality. I try to talk
of everything being ok but it doesn't help. Now they think
I'm against them and I'm trying to coherse them.
Paranoia in these states can get very ugly. Your best
friend can turn into a sadistic FBI agent in two seconds.

It seems like being out side has calmed them down a bit
or maybe the hours are taking care of it. When your
tripping real hard time does very strange things. It will fly
by and without warning jerk to a complete halt. but the
sun is making its presence known and we have to get
back to Ohio soon. We walk down to check on the car
before we leave but guess what. NO CAR. Holy fuck, the
car has been towed from the location Natas had left it.
Gone. Now three people totally out of their minds have to
walk to the police station and try and get the car out of
the impound. Splendid.

We begin our walk through the big apple, laced to the
gills. I have a book of acid and quarter pound of weed in
my backpack (of course I had to hold the shit). The two
girls perfectly out of their minds with me walking through
the streets of new york. Not to mention we are heading to
the police station. Christine is supposed to be trying out
for a "Hair" audition today and is now busting into an acid
hymn of "age of Aquarius" at the top of her lungs. She
dances from one side of the street to the next delivering
each verse with joyful abandon. The graffiti on the walls
takes on the tone of futuristic Aztec style scrawling.
Waves of animated verse smashing and swirling in

rainbows of neon sludge . The art drips from the walls into my minds cortex, blending reality and fantasy into a mud pie.

We arrive at the station as Tena takes off inside. I am not going there to save my life(considering the back pack that I was wearing could get me 20 years in prison),so I post up and wait for the sentence that awaits. I was pretty sure I would never see them again and they would be coming for me soon enough. Christine is still singing and dancing as Tena reemerges from the police station with more looks of frustration.

"We have to go to the impound to get the car" she says with a whimper.

"I have no proof that the car is mine, I don't know what we are going to do".

Well lets go and face the music at the impound. It wasn't long until we were at the impound, a little mobile home shack in the middle of a parking lot.

"good luck" I tell Tena as she enters the compound.

The place looks like something out of a war zone.

Barbed wire, homeless people, junk, trash, filth. Tena comes back out with relief on her face.

"They weren't even speaking English in there" she explains with a shit eating grin. "I don't know how but I got the car back".

No license, no title, no mind, and they let her have it back. I guess the universe is going to give us a break. Get out of here was the message I got.

After getting into the car the girls decide its a bad idea to go back to the apartment. Christine's boyfriend was still there and they were not even close to being down yet from the last hits they took. We drive up north of the city and find some solitude in the fresh air and vegetation. They decide we should get a room, but the rooms are way to pricey in the city. We head over the river to jersey. We find a beat up little hole in the wall and get a room. Now most guys would be very excited to be getting a room with two hot chicks, but to tell you the truth, it was the last thing on my ravished mind. All I want is sleep at this point. They kindly say I can sleep in one of the beds and they would share but I decline for the floor. We all smell worse than anything you could imagine. Like something just crawled out of the sewer and took a dump on all our heads. Exhaustion has completely taking over. I just lay on the floor and fall into darkness. Rest beautiful rest.

Chapter 4

Top of the hill

We awoke from our slumber just in time to shower and check out. My clothes smell of sewer ,so they have to be thrown away. Everyone is feeling very strung out and I know I'm still tripping a bit. Things are quiet in the car driving back into the city. After what just happen last night there isn't much to say. We drive back to one of Christine's friends house (since i don't think I'm very welcome back at the devil den) and we smoke a little before the long ride back. "the red" stops by to see how everything panned out(probably to see if we actually made it out alive).He breaks out some different type of herb called "aura" and packs up some hits. The smoke is smooth and cools the throat. Some how Tena and I decided it would be a good idea to drop some more hits of "magik" before we hit the road. We are still tripping from last night ,so 3 shouldn't do to much to us now. We chomp them down with no delay, as worried looks are passed around the room. Oh well why start being responsible now? We say our final goodbyes and take off down the road to Ohio.

The trip starts off with pouring rain that seems to be turning into a fucking hurricane. Of course the intensity of the rain is most probably due to the acid we are on.

"It feels the car is driving itself" Tena states "I'm pretty sure I can take my hands off the wheel and it will drive itself" as she slowly takes both hands off the wheel.

And low and behold the car is shooting through Niagara falls with no one driving but Tena's brain.

"Are you nuts, get your hands back on the wheel" I exclaim with sheer panic.

She slowly puts her hands back on the wheel with a sinister smile. Man this chick is crazy but i love it. One thing we have totally over looked is that we have spent all our money on drugs and now have no money for gas or tolls for the next 5 hours. We had enough to get out of new york proper but there is still the turnpike tolls and we are starting to run out of gas. Some how in the adventure the rain stops and starts to take on the form of snow. We must be heading north east instead of south east. No map of course just a "go with it" attitude that the universe is leading us down the right path. and now we are no where near civilization,. We begin coasting up and down icy country roads trying to hold on to the last bit of gas we have. Where the fuck did the freeway go? How did we get so fucking off track. The gas gage is dropping fast as we slip down mountainous roads of sheer ice. Dread is setting in for both of us since we have no winter clothes and we are about to be out of gas. Finally out of nowhere we see a snow covered gas station off in the distance. Hope. Thank god we are not going to freeze to death in north west new york. but hold up, we have no fucking money what so ever. Tena goes in and I wait in the car. What is she going to tell this poor clerk. Tena emerges from the station with a smile.

"I just told the guy our situation, we have no money and we have to get gas. You can call the cops on us but we cant pay for the gas" she explains.

"He just said to get out of here as fast as we can and take the gas you need".

Holy crap, the universe is a funny place. We fill up and take off into the snow. The only thing is the gas isn't going to get us home. Not even close. So we make a plan to shoot through Pittsburgh and sell some of our wears. I know a few people in there (since my cosmic striptease in July). I know there has to be a party happening. The plan was to sell enough acid to at least get some dam gas home. We get word from two guys who had helped me through the night at tunnel vision.

Doogie and Steve were their names. We headed over to their apartment to chill a bit before heading out to sell our goods.

The apartment building was old and brick with crawling vines encompassing with entire building. It looked like artists were taking up most of the residence. We made our way up some little stairs that ran up the back. I knocked on the old wooden door that looked like it hadn't been replaced since the early 1900s. The door flies open with Steve's roar right behind.

"Hey it's the naked guy, glad to see you found your clothes" he laughs as he hugs the both of us with a raver death grip.

"Come in come in so happy to you see you guys made it."

The inside of the apartment walls are covered with flyers and posters of events from around the globe. There are two small futons that wrap around the ceremonial coffee table covered in every weed accessory known to mankind. Doogie is sitting at the decks spinning trance records unaware we have stepped in.

"Sit, sit, how are you doing, man you had us really

worried at the show. You were totally out of it, it took like six HUGE guys to hold you down. We thought you were going to die for sure. What the hell were you on?" Steve states grabbing a 4 foot bong from behind one of the futons.

"Well I thought it was ten but turned out to be 40."

I embarrassingly exclaim grabbing some of the skunk from our bag of tricks.

"Holy shit that's a big difference, you have to be careful when you go messing with acid. There is such a huge variation in how strong each kind is. Each one can be a world of difference."

Steve has been throwing parties for two years and was one of the main promoters behind Tunnel Vision. He was 20 something full of the ideals of the rave scene. Very open and kind. Laid back semi professional artist that still believed in every bone of his body that we were making a difference. Even if that only meant providing a place for people to gather and dance until the sun comes up. Very simple but very important.

"So you brought some Magik paper for me to check out right?" rubbing his sweating hands together.

"Oh I sure did and your going to love em" pulling out one of the handsome sheets from my bag.

I cut him off three to try out (thinking HE might want to also buy some) and pack up the four footer.

Doogie puts on a cd and comes over with smiles and hugs.

"Hey there naked guy ,glad to see your still in one piece there buddy" he smirks with a slight sarcastic hint.

" Yea ,Yea I've heard it a few times now" as I hand him the bong to quiet up the situation.

Steve thought it would be a good idea to go up to the roof and check out the night sky. Within a few minutes of getting up there Steve was pulling out flyers from months ago. In his state of now fully tripping, he forgot that these parties had already happened. He started calling info lines, thinking he was helping us get to one of these past events. Man this acid is powerful. This guy is a head and he is being transported to other times in the past through his mind. Fucking heavy. We quickly made our goodbyes and headed out to a underground Doogie had suggested. Hopefully to make some money and get home. We didn't even think that maybe we wouldn't be welcome.

What, two strange people show up out of nowhere and need to sell off some really good acid for really cheap to get gas home. Yea right.

We sailed through downtown Pittsburgh to an abandon strip mall that from the looks of it hadn't been used in decades. The party looked pretty packed from the parking lot and the usual crew of freaks, geeks and dealers were hanging around the entrance. The people at the event didn't seem to take to our sales idea very well, especially the drug dealers who were already working the event.

"Maybe you guys should just get out of here" states one of the dealers with a stern "get the fuck away from us look.

"We cant help you at all".

Well, this is perfect, so much for the vibe of our brothers when someone is in need. We leave completely out of ideas of what to do. We have no money and no gas and no where else to turn. We drive out of the parking lot and see a BP gas station very near us. So I guess that's where we are going to run out of gas. As we pull up, we see the attendant looks like he just got done at a dead show. Hipped out to the max. Tena comes up with a plan.

"Lets bribe the deadhead with acid to fill up the car" she giggles to herself.

She walks up to the glass and states our position. low and behold the doors fly open and a very excited hippy is giving us the treatment.

"You guys take whatever you need, food, drinks, smokes, gas whatever just take what you need".

We are overwhelmed with sheer happiness. This guy could have called the cops or just said no but acid talks and he wanted some real bad. "I cant believe this" he cheers "Me and my friends look all over for this stuff."

We cut him out a 20 strip(about 100 dollars worth) and fill up our ship. Angels do exist and we just got to meet one(or just another desperate drug addict looking for a fix) Now we have enough gas to get home.

See you later Pittsburgh hello C-bus.

We finally got back to our little city of Columbus. Oh how so much has changed in just a few days. This city is getting smaller by the hour. We are now starting to come down from our 4 day acid trip and things are getting hairy to stay the least. Paranoia doesn't come close to this state of mind. Every car takes the appearance of a undercover vehicle. With every glance out of the window the scene gets more sinister. We decide not to go home because that's the first place they would expect us to go. The heats on, they know what's up, we are totally fucked. Waves of intense fear and loathing. We end up at a little shit hole hotel walled up and not answering phones. Our friend Tim stops by and we try to explain our dilemma.

"look man, look at that car its federal, I know it" I feverishly explain.

He gives the long drawn out "holy shit this guy has lost his marbles" look and knows I'm out to lunch hard. I ignore it as "he just doesn't know" moment and peer out the blinds waiting for the next vehicle to massacre my mind with panic. Tim departs not soon after and now its time to deal with this. As soon as we leave we know there will be a tail so we have to get rid of the goods right away. Where can we go, who can we trust. Tena calls her aunt. She agrees to help Tena and we head out. Our plan is to flush the rest of the acid that we had. Now remember this is all a delusion of our minds, so we thought. We were actually sorely mistaken. We spoke to no one about our plans. no one. but now Tena's aunt knew so we had to act fast. Trust no one. We arrive at Tena's aunts and are greeted with more very worried looks. Joyce, Tena's aunt, takes Tena into a back bedroom with the stash. I stayed in the living room. some how subconsciously I just couldn't watch that beautifully vicious drug be destroyed.

From Tena's account they ripped every sheet up into little pieces and flushed them down the toilet. Mission complete. now to the people who just lent us 2,000 dollars for drugs we just flushed down the toilet. Run for the hills.

I knew two teachers from my junior high days who lived out in the sticks. They agreed to let us stay the night while we got our heads straight. These were the coolest people on earth. In junior high they let me come and stay at their cabin when I was a bit suicidal. I had done a little therapy and had never really got over very severe childhood memories of being dragged out of bed by a pulsating green globe of light. I would be dragged past my sleeping parents screaming at the top of my paralyzed lungs to my parents deaf ears. It would drag me up into our attic and then I cant recall anymore. Once faced with something like this as a kid, your perception of reality changes permantley. You come to the realization that there are things that even your parents cant save you from. The feeling of total terror and pain. Being forced by an unknown source out of your parental dome of security. Trust, pain, loyalty, love, sleep, normality all seem alien in nature. Well besides all that, it surfaced as a want to kill myself in my later years.

They helped me and now I know they would at least give us a safe place to rest that no one ever knew about. They courted us without much questions seeing the wear on our faces. I have no idea the last time we slept. we couldn't even see how tired we were. There was only one bed, so we had to share. We had started to become very close over the past weeks but we still hadn't crossed that boundary. And it wasn't happening tonight. Clothes remained on but the few centimeters between us felt like a mile. We were so close yet so far away.

"Your birthday is on Halloween, we should go to the Smokey mountains" I whisper to her.

"Sounds good we are going to need some acid" she slights back falling asleep.

One of our friends some how got a hold of some more Magic(don't ask me how because I still haven't figured that one out) and gave Tena 10 hits for her birthday. We were going to go to the Smokey mountains on an Cherokee Indian reservation. Oh did I mention her birthday was on Halloween. that's right folks all hallows eve. So I thought it would be a good idea to drop acid on top of a mountain on Halloween. Perfect idea. We head down to Tennessee from Columbus and drive straight up to the highest peak on the reservation. The sun was going down fast and most of the cars were heading away from the reservation. This is a perfect spot. Darkness sets in and we drop our five hits a piece. We are both a bit tired from the ride ,so a nap is decided upon. We will be tripping when we wake. Then we can go out and adventure into the starry night. Just for extra spiritual precaution, I burn some ceremonial herbs giving to me from an urban shaman I had met recently. He told me to place them on or around the area that we would be tripping. I lit the herbs and placed them on the windshield of the car.

We lay our seats back and start our attempt at a nap. My mind starts to gel and I can tell I wont be sleeping at all tonight. For the better, ill just let Tena rest. The whole night lay before us. And as I sit there in my wandering lsd blotted mind, I hear a stir on Tena's side of the car. She seems asleep but its not restful at all. Slowly as if oil seeping from the mount of Golgotha, a slight laughter seeps from Tena. A laughter so cynical so purely evil it could shake you out of your underwear.

"HA HA HA" growls the voice as Tena begins to become erect.

As she turns and sits up to face me I notice her face begin to shift and layer out in a hall of mirrors effect. I could see one face layered on top of another. Faces of all the evil creatures that have ever existed. Hitler to Mason to Mau to Leviathan to Belial to demons with no names. The faces began to solidify down to one semi ghostly appearance. Her face elongated and grew a pointed beard. Rounded spectacles formed around the rim of her face. Her hair became sheer black and grew around her neck. All the while laughing from the oily pits.

"Why would you care of such humans, they are so weak and pathetic" growls the demon from within Tena's body.

Fuck me ,now I'm fucking terrified. Tena has been totally possessed by the master of the deep. Time to bolt. Shit has hit the fan real bad. I go for the keys and crank the ignition. Wub wub wubbbwubbbbb. The battery is totally dead. Holy crap. This amuses the demon to no end.

"There is no escape from here, you cannot run" it seethes.

I really did it this time.

I grabbed the wheel and began to cry. and i mean i cried like a baby. I cried for the dear lord god almighty any where in this universe to help me please. While I'm dripping rivers of tears, the car is slowly engulfed in a huge thunder cloud. It slowly comes in from the horizon and takes over the whole top of the mountain. You couldn't see two inches in front of the car. So I guess running is out. That was the next step already foreseen by the demon. During this time I tried not to even look in Tena's direction. It was much to terrifying after the last face of killer thing.

"You know you could kill her right now, no one would know, you could take her right now" tempted whatever I was dealing with.

The floor of the car dissolves into sheer darkness. "Tena" and I are now sitting perched on the edge of a rocky rim which circles a bottomless pit. Tena's face is a very deep pale white and her hair has grown longer to wrap around her feet. Wings have extended out of her back and fold down to her sides.

"Why would you want to save such a race? Even if you had the power? Why would you bother? questioned the demon.

"Of course ,I would" I wept grabbing onto the steering wheel, which was the only thing holding me from slipping into the bottomless pit.

"God loves the human race" I cried trying to convince myself of anything in the face of pure evil.

"Please God, please help me" as the tears fell harder and the laughter grows deeper.

Then at the moment of total mental collapse, a single ray of light pierces through the predawn clouds. A ray of light straight from the belly of heaven.

A saving ray of humanity. The clouds began to spread like the red sea. Tena throws open the door and violently projects green vomit everywhere.

"What happened" she questions with a very startled look as she wipes the goo from her face.

"Don't worry about it" i murmur wiping away the tears from my face. "Lets get some air".

The clouds were pushing back fast as the early sunrise blasted onto the mountain top. I am still tripping very hard. We walk out to the ridge of the mountain and view the staggering heights we are at. The whole of the Smokey mountain range lay out before us. A huge black crow swoops out of the sky and lands right next to us. It doesn't seem like a bird at all but a great watcher of the sky. Tena and I embrace, hugging each other like there was no other thing in the world. We hadn't really ever touched in a affectionate way until this moment but the tension had been building for weeks now. Now we were getting closer to being a couple then ever before.

I feel the love flowing between us, like a river flooding over a dam. I decide we both need to get grounded to the planet, really connect with mother earth and feel the vibrations of an ancient peoples land. I have some Shawnee blood, so I hold the native American tribes in very high regard. Tena gives me some weird looks(she wasn't conscious for what I just went through) as I grab my tape player and head for a higher ridge laying out over a cliff face. Tena heads off a little to my right. I put on the headphones and start the tape of Keoki. The mix was called "All Mixed Up". Keoki was like a prophet to us in the underground. His mixes felt like he had been to where we wanted to go. To that place that few had ever seen. He gave us hope for a better future. It was a very tribal mix that fit well with my motives of planetary connection. "Let me take you on a journeyyyyyy" pulses Ursula Rucker's beautiful voice. The sound is so divine it sounds like it was coming out of the sky. I sit Indian style with the beats drifting over my mind as I view out over the huge valley expanding out below. The earth's vibrations flowing up from the planet into my bloodstream up into my crown chakra. A deep sense of peace washes over my body as the sun begins to warm the air around me. Samadhi has been reached.

We return to the car growing quickly aware we are still stuck on top of a mountain with a dead car battery. A great finish to a hellish night. Out of nowhere we notice a black van that must have pulled up while we were on the ridge. Some brightly covered individuals were piling out of the back. maybe they have some jumper cables. Oh please let us get off this mountain. Tena goes over and begins to try and ask these strange people if they can give us a jump. One of the guys in the group of three starts to talk to the others in a completely foreign language. It sounds like German. Great the only help we have up here and they don't even speak English.

Fucking awesome. With a series of hand gestures and swinging we get the point across of what we need. They did have cables and did jump the car. Finally we can get off this mountain. We begin our descent out of the heavens and down to ground level earth. We pull over at the side of the road which rests next to a mountainous river. We have a little sacred herb left and Tena takes out her little brass smoking pipe.

We puff magical clouds of smoke over the water as we begin to slowly get grounded from our experiences of last night. The river pulses with our breath, calms the nerves of very weary hyperspace travelers. We hit the main freeway as the sun is setting into the distance. The first stars break through the dusky twilight as i push up the highway. I open the sunroof to a blast of cool October air. Tena drifts to sleep as my mind sails through the starry fall sky.

Chapter 5

Down Hill Follies

The weeks begin to move slowly along as the winter sets in. Our dope dealing has been growing fast. We had started moving green in weight to try and make money since we both had quit our jobs. We were also selling acid all over the place. Usually we would show up very early in the morning, when no one would expect us. On one of those particular mornings we had just dropped of some hits to a guy on OSU's campus and were feeling pretty good about ourselves. We decided it would be really good to get out of the city and go to old mans cave state park. Just trip out, smoke some X and get connected to the earth. I know, we spend a lot of time "getting reconnected" to our planet. We held this process in highest regard. Feeling allied with the forces of nature. Giving thanks that we were able to live in this beautiful world by getting totally wrecked on as many drugs as possible. We dropped a few hits of acid for the road for good measure and headed out on the freeway east. We had a half pound of green, a few x tabs and a few hits of L. Dee lite's "dew drops in the garden" flowed out of car speakers with soothing loving rhythms. It was winter but we felt no cold. In Tena's spaceship the weather was just fine. Then out of nowhere, of course, the disco lights came blazing. Statey is right behind us, pulling us over. Perfect. We are cosmically fucked. Again.

As he runs his pre screen, I am sitting in the passenger seat totally frozen. Our tags are expired, we are both tripping our faces off, I have a half pound of green in my lap, with x and Tena's holding L.

This is it, we are going to jail for sure. There's no laughter or quick exit. I state highway officer is coming to the car and we are fucked.

" Mme, do you know your tags are expired" the cop uniformly states.

" Yes, I do. I'm going to take care of them as soon as we go home, I'm so sorry" Tena slyly smears to the cop with her best "I'm an innocent girl " look.

"Can you please come with me Mrs. Zansouten" as he opens the door of the car.

I feel my life coming to an end. I'm going to jail for at least two years. At least. Time comes to a complete halt. Tena is escorted to the back of the cruiser. The cop takes out her purse and begins to look inside. Holy shit the acid is in there.

" Hey you cant do that" Tena exclaims to the officer. " What?" propels the officer.

" Well you cant just go searching through people's purses for no reason" pipes back Tena like only she can.

The cop almost subconsciously, by the look of it , puts the belongings back in her purse.

"Get in the back of the car" states the cop.

Oh that's it. Holy shit on me. She's getting hemmed up and I'm next. More sinking stomach mess. Tena sits in the back of the cruiser as things get a bit weird. From what Tena had told me the officer seemed to be externally controlled for a brief time by an off world being. "off world" meaning not of this physical realm.

"What do you want me to do" calmly states the new inhabitant of this officers body.

"I just want to get out of this car and go" Tena vollies back. "whatever i need to do to just go".

"There are more of my kind the way you are going"

"It would be better for you just to go home" shoots the officer as he hands back Tena's license back to her.

All the while mind you I'm still in the car waiting to go to prison. Tena returns to the car pale as a ghost and proceeds to make a left and head back to town.

"What the fuck happened" I nervously quivered still recovering from our brush with the man.

"Ill explain later" she murmurs, not even wanting to dive into what just really happened.

This was the first 30 minutes of this acid trip and things just kept getting more intense. We were falling completely out of control. The acid was coming on strong. We stopped at a gas station on the way to my house and sat out in a little cut of grass under a tree. I was watching this beam of light shine out of the top of Tena's head. A ray of light was coming right out of the crown of her head. We embraced and I felt her love flowing through my bones. The whole planet has an energy that literally binds us to everything. Its been there since you were born and that's why the older we get the more we forget about its presence.

I felt this connected energy elegantly moving through Tena. One energy field, one continuous being with two parts flowing in and out of a whole.

Tena began to tell me what was on her mind. She was thinking that Satan was once an angel of god. He was held above all others in the choir of high. Because of this all Satan has to do is ask for forgiveness from god then he will be allowed back into heaven. This action will end the whole existence of hell, uniting heaven and hell into one Eden of paradise. All Satan has to do is break his ego down and bow before the almighty. She tells me that we needed to trip with Satan. She is convinced we had the power to save his soul.

Tena has derived that "Eric the red" is the embodiment of Satan. He has the magik acid that warped our minds into oblivion. He is the guy we were looking for.

For us to trip with Satan, we needed to make a long distance call to new york. That's a lot of quarters. We needed to go to my house and use the phone. Since both my parents are home it shouldn't be a problem to make a quick call to Satan. We pull out of the gas station and head for my parents house a few minutes away. I notice that there is a car following us. Holy fuck there it is again. in front of us going the other way. I swear that's the same fucking car and driver. Holy shit that felt like a dimensional shift of some kind. Tripping. Tripping hard. We pull up to the house with the promise from Tena she was going to be cool.

"I promise" she states with what seemed to be sincerity.

We walk up to the front door and low and beheld its locked.

"Just knock" i say knowing that my parents where home.

Instead of knocking on the door, Tena smashes her hand

right through the glass.

"My energy did it" she explained with no blood or cuts whatsoever. "I swear it was the energy, it just shattered from my energy".

I sure hope my mom and dad understand the power of the force.

My mom and dad come down the stairs after hearing the loud shatter of glass hitting the kitchen floor.

"What is going on" my mom shouts with complete astonishment and fear.

My dad slowly follows having a hard time walking. My parents are both very over weight and both had constant problems with their hearts and health. Tena calmly sits down on a chair next to my parents and proceeds to tell them our side of "things".

"You see, we need to trip with Satan. If we can get him to realize he can be forgiven, he can get back into heaven. God forgives all and that's all he has to do ,its that simple" she states with the firmest of confidence.

I had to admit at the time she had a very valid point from the Judea- Christian point of view, even though blasphemous to the church she was raised in. My parents faces become even more worried with every word.

"Are you on something?" My mom asks already knowing the answer. "Yes , we are on acid but if you took some to, you would be able to

see" Tena shyly states with perceived honest intent.

Holy shit, now things are going way to fucking far. My parents who already have heart conditions, look at present as if they are both going to drop dead in front of us. I grabbed Tena and headed for the office upstairs. Now we must contact Satan , who happens to be a homeless drug dealer that lives in nyc.

Tena proceeds to dial up "the red" ,while I soak in what's going on. It feels like a cosmic orchestra is playing out in real time reality. I look toward the ceiling and it gently disappears into waves of shimmering indigo oceans. A form begins to appear in the shape of what looks like a human man floating in this indigo space field.

"Eric, this is Tena" pause "we need to come to new york and save your soul, you can get back into heaven".

Mr Eric is totally unaware he was Satan ,or that he needed saved in anyway.

"How much did you take" Eric replies with a unshaken tone. "You need to chill out and stop tripping for a while little one" he states before kindly excusing himself off the phone.

We both start to chill out and obviously start to sober up just a bit. Enough to realize my front door window is smashed and my mom is ready to call the police on us. Time to split this scene and fast. We headed for our hide away, the dam. The dam was a sacred place to our trips. Usually no one came out to the dam after the sun went down, so you could hang out or crash all night and not be bothered. It was a huge spaceship looking reservoir with lake on one side and a stream on the other side where it was dammed off. It had a little park and a lookout that he climbed during summer months. Well it wasn't summer, it was the dead of winter and about a foot of snow on the ground. and much more steadily flowing from the heavens. We'll be fine, we will rest for a couple of hours and go find a place to stay. No problem .Its very peaceful with not a car in sight. So quiet. The wind slowly wipes up against the car, slowly rocking it back in forth. We begin to drift off into the white space of pure calm. Leave the car on, few hours, no more. So warm. Drifting , just blowing in the warm air of the car.

As we slowly drifted to sleep, the snow began to fall harder and harder. Falling so hard you couldn't really see in front of the car. Tena was already asleep and i was getting there. Off in the distance a noticed a form appearing out of the snow wall. I squinted to try and see what the hell would be out here in a snow storm. It was very faint, about 3 foot tall all white with glowing black eyes. What the fuck is that, as I begin to become more awake or now fully dreaming. I'm fading out. Hold on wait. what is it......Then a rapid tapping at the window. TAP TAP TAP. It was getting louder quick. I must have falling totally asleep(I cant remember anything since the sighting which seemed to be a few seconds ago). I moved my seat to an upright position(don't know how the fuck that happened, I was fully upright before the missing time) and noticed a light being shown through the window. TAP TAP TAP TAP. Its getting very loud now with a voice behind it.

"Roll your window down" came a muffled voice from the light. I rolled the window down as snow fell in.

"What the hell do you think your doing out here"

exclaimed a very pissed off police officer.

"You can die of carbon monoxide poisoning sleeping out here like this, are you fucking nuts".

Well not at this point, i was dead sober considering we still have all the drugs from the day on us and now there are cops at the door.

"We were just going to rest for a second and we must have been out here longer than we had expected".I shuffled off to the calling cop.

He must have been prepared for the worst expecting to find dead bodies or something.

"Don't you have anywhere to go?" stated the officer.

"Yes we do(no we didn't) and we will head there right now, sorry for the trouble officer" as i slowly went to roll up the window.

"Well then get there and don't pull this shit again" faded the officers voice from the now leaving cruiser.

Tena had a friend near and we just needed a place to crash for a bit. We had a big deal going down with some green tomorrow and we should be getting some money from that.

Tena's friend was a very sweet girl by the name of Danny. She let us in with no questions asked and we posted up on the floor of an empty bedroom. To be truthful it could have been the sidewalk at this point. Complete exhaustion was setting in. We were meeting with our green dealer, Mickey ,in a few hours and we needed some rest. It was a big shipment this time(10 lbs) and we couldn't miss it.

We both lay down on the floor and wrapped our arms around each other. We were spiraling out of control and we both knew it. but we didn't care. We were on the bus and taking this ride to the end of time. Nothing mattered but creating an evolution of the mind for the whole world. Turn on the planet to wake up. To wake the youth of today and let them know they have the power to change everything. To open minds all the way. To bring about a dancing orgy of global peace. The floor began to soften as it does right before sleeping on a hard surface. It almost feels like rubber, as we drifted off to sleep. This time inside.

Today we are meeting with our green dealer, Mickey. He lives in a affluent part of Columbus called weterville. I think he is still living with his parents, even though he makes great money. and was well into his thirties.

Kind of strange but we are getting used to strange. Almost making it a way of life. We show up and walk up a pathway to the beautiful estate. He greats us with large welcomes and leads us into the living room.

"Well you guys have been doing good ,so we're going to go ahead a front you the 10 at 25 a piece".

Well now, that's a lot of weed. and we are supposed to have one buyer so this should go smooth. Tena grew up with the buyer and seems trust worthy. Mickey leaves for a second and returns with a big red cooler.

"Here ya go, its your ass if something happens" he gleams with a smile.

I open the cooler to find 10 neatly packaged bags of emerald green herb.

"How long before I get that cheese back" Mickey asks throwing out two 8 balls of what seemed to be coke out on the couch.

"4 or five days tops" retorts Tena. "what's that" pointing at the balls on the couch.

"I thought you guys might be down to sell some of this too" as Mickey slips back into his recliner".

"Actually no we don't mess with anything like that" Tena pipes back heading for the door with me and the cooler in tow. "Ill see you soon and remember, its your ass" as the door shuts behind me.

Now we were off to Sam's house. He lived over in the not so affluent side of town of burgville. That's where i was from. Not that it was bad ,it was a far cry from where we used to live growing up, it was just very boring. and i mean very. Sam was one of Tena's school mates back in the day as they say and had kept in contact with her ever since. He was the one taking the weight from us at 3 a piece, so we would be making 500 on each, so 5,000 grand to us for the job well done. We show up with cooler in tow and walk up the snowy hill to the door. He greats us with big hello's and hugs. We proceed to the living room and test out the merch. Beautiful sticky lime green bud fills the nostrils with the fragrance of a candy skunk.

"Wow" smiles Sam knowing this is going to bring some steady profits. "I think we should take some acid to celebrate" I state whipping out some blotter. "Ill pass" states Sam.

"I still have to drive and go get the money for this. I have to take half with me and ill get the other half when i come back and pay you".

We are at this dudes house, where is he going to go.

"Sure, no problem" as i munch down two hits and hand some to Tena.

She doesn't even hesitate and slides the paper onto her tongue.

"When i get back we should go watch "powder" while you guys are tripping." states Sam.

I started to notice the acid creeping in. The walls starting to move in wave forms. The feeling of trying to maintain normal functioning but getting harder by the second.

"Ill be back in like 30 minutes with the rest of the money, see you soon" as Sam and his very quiet girlfriend I hadn't notice before now walked out the door with a bag of 5.

We had the rest with us in the cooler. We sat down on the couch and started packing up bong loads in Sam's three footer. The weed would slow down the now raging acid we had consumed not 1 hour ago. We just tripped like 2 days ago or was it yesterday, well who knows. We should have a good tolerance going, so i didn't think it would be hitting us that hard.5,6,7 good tokes and everything smoothed out a bit. Time began to slide and everything was getting gooey. Then the phone starts ringing. Its Sam's phone, so I'm sure as shitting not answering it. The message machine picks up and its Sam's girlfriend.

"Pick up you guys, Sam is in trouble and I have to talk to

you now, please pick up". Tena runs to the phone.

"Sam just got busted and they are coming to the house, get out now" pants Sam's girlfriend.

"They are coming, get out right now!!!".

We hit the ground running with cooler in tow. Jumped in Tena's car and started getting real fucking panicked.

"What the fuck do we do now, they could have the roads blocked off already, they could have the patrol already prepared for us to run, what the fuck do we do" i scream at Tena as we whip down Sam's road.

"Get rid of the L and ill find a place to stash the cooler" i state to Tena as she hangs out the door dropping hits of L all over the road.

I found a construction site that looked pretty much left alone and hid the cooler under a huge tarp.

"We'll get it tomorrow, we have to get out of town now" as my foot hits the gas and I head out the exact opposite direction of town.

I drove and drove until we saw a Best Western a good 2 hours out of town. We had no money and just got ripped off for 25,000.and we were still tripping hardcore. If we don't have that money to Mickey in 4 days we are dead. no questions. we get a room with some hefty stares. We get to the room and begin to think how to get out of this mess. If we call Mickey, he wont believe a word. There is no way of getting 25,000 in 4 days. We are both practically homeless and our parents don't have anywhere near that kind of loot. The acid was still humming in our minds as we tried to see a path where we didn't end up dying. This contemplation went on until we noticed the sun peering through the blinds. There is only one solution. Get the fuck way out of town as soon as possible.

To get out of town we needed money and we needed it fast. We had fronted out some herb to a couple of Tena's friends, so we had some loot coming back from that. All we had to do is get back into town and pick up the money. We decided that we should go to Chicago, to an event called "Save the Robots". That's what we were, robots, and we definitely needed saving. When your on acid all the time you really start to think everything is happening for a reason. Names take on special meaning as does everything else that most people look over or ignore. You start to go with this "universal flow" that you have no choice to follow. No matter how many people tell you "you are nuts",it doesn't matter because to you they are the ones who have lost their minds. Your following your destiny. Nothing else matters. In the acid reality everything takes on a "all or nothing" type of atmosphere. Everything is big and important on acid. No detail goes unnoticed and everything is blown WAY out of normal everyday proportion. Thus thinking that "Save the Robots" was directed right at us.

Must be what the universe has in store, so nothing else to do but go with it and hope for the best.

We made it over to Jason and Ryan's house(Tena's friends) and were greeted with the usual niceties. They were two college kids who had great weed and were very reliable as far as drug dealers are concerned. Needless to say they were a little concerned about our plans to be saved in Chicago, not to mention we had been tripping for weeks(or months who knows at this point).They had 800 for us and an ounce left over. Perfect, just enough to get us to Chicago and get saved. We chatted a while longer on how we thought everyone should be on acid and that we had evolved beyond food. All we needed was some acid, orange juice and a rave. What else was there? With more strange looks from our audience we decided it was time to hit the street. So at this point we had just been ripped off for 5 lbs, owed 25,000 to a killing drug dealer, and were about to go to Chicago on the only money and drugs we had left to go to a rave. Off to the windy city we go.

Chapter 6

Chi-town Contact

We hit the road from Columbus feeling some of the fear start to leave the atmosphere. The highway always seemed best. Always moving. Harder to track. Out of sight out of my mind i guess. I compulsively rolled joints all the way up the highway. The thick green smoke washed away some of the nervousness away. At least for the time being. We didn't speak much, just let the smoke roll in an eerie silence. The party we were going to featured one of the biggest djs on earth. Derek May. Grandfather of the techno scene and known for his outer space dj sets. Kevin Sanderson, Juan Atkins ,and himself formed the Detroit techno sound. Unlike most that think of Detroit techno as being a very hard punishing sound, the early forefathers had a lot of funk and soul to their music.

They were from Motown. They got their sounds and yearnings from early funk tracks and put a technologic edge to it. He was playing an extended 6 hour set and it made for a good distraction to say the least. We had been to Chicago a few times for some of the best parties on earth at the time. Mike Dearborn was still doing "Majesty" events.4,000 ravers heads down and dancing their asses off to Martin Luther King "I have a dream" remixed by Dearborn into a mutant alien train headed for the tops of heaven. The Planet D-Jax events would also happen every lucky moon. Vibeanuts held it down at some of the sickest rollerink raves imaginable. Full on Chicago raving glory days. Chicago has very loyal fans of dance music and much love for the scene that created the sound we call house today. A lot of history in the sidewalks of this great city.

We had no idea where to go or where we were at all to tell you the truth. We had the info line for the event and not much else. It was Saturday so all the hotels in the city are booked solid. We found one hotel that still had rooms but the rooms were 250.00 a night. What the hell, we have 600 to last us to whenever but lets get a 250 dollar luxury room. Fuck it. We walked into the lobby and were surrounded by pristine beauty. The hotel was beautiful from top to bottom with a bunch of priests running around inside. What the fuck is going on. Why all the priests. Did they know we were coming for Christs sake!

"Hello, yes you'll have to excuse all the ruckus. There is a priest convention in the hotel. your floor is the only floor that isn't filled with priests" exclaims the desk attendant with a smug grin.

From the look of us I think she could tell we were not here for the convention. and from the look of the priests they were not to happy with our presence either. or could it be we smell like a skunk's intestine after 6 hours of chain smoking the herb.

We make it up to the beautiful room with a view to die for. You could see the Chicago skyline spread out against frozen lake Michigan. Stunning. We lay out our bags and I make the call to the info line to get the map point. It looks like the spot is not to far from the hotel, so we have enough time to smoke another joint and head out into the wild streets of chi town. Its freezing like only freezing can happen in Chicago. Its the kinda cold that shoots right through to your bones. No escaping it. We find our way over to the map point which at this point consisted of a parking lot full of ravers. Lines of cars running waiting for something. Then as we parked the car, out of the alley pulls a gray school bus. A very ominous looking school bus for that matter. Very beat up with fully blackened windows.

We are shuffled onto the bus with a group of about 20 others and away we flew. You couldn't look out the windows and the bus was floating down many twists and turns at speed. It felt as if we were running from something. Or maybe this is this guy's route and he knows it like the back of his hand. He would fly over huge humps then stop at what would feel like an alley. He was an older gruffy fellow looking very pissed to be spending his Saturday evening driving a bunch of party going kids to underground freak-outs. You could almost see out the front at times but as soon as you think you had a good enough hold to take a look he would jerk the wheel and smash back down another jagged street. Tena was still freezing, so i grabbed onto her shivering body and hoped to land safely. We were very worried about all the events we left behind, not knowing anything that was going on. Good or bad. We knew people were looking for us but we knew they wouldn't be looking here. Needless to say paranoia was still a Huge factor. We just got put on a bus that we hoped is going to the event and not straight to the police station. and from the looks of the rest of the travelers, im not the only one thinking it.

The blackened bus rips to a stop and the doors of the bus fly open. "everybody out" pipes the bus driver.

We start to shuffle out onto the sidewalk in front of a huge building. It looked very empty for a Chicago party. No one was in line or standing out front. Just two huge closed doors and us. Then as fast as the bus came, it disappeared into the night. As the bus pulled away the doors of the building flew open.

We were greeted by swat uniforms and machine guns. All branded with the all to familiar logo "D.E.A".Holy fuck. This is a set up. Huge paramilitary monsters with flash lights, bullet proof vests, riot masks, and full on machine guns shove the pack into the building as the doors are closed behind us. The agents seem to be the security for the event. At least that's what it looks like. They proceed to give us the full pat down search treatment. Check the crotch, belt loops, cuffs, sweater, shoes. Huge walk in metal detectors hang over our heads as we get frisked by the storm troopers. From the looks of their confiscation buckets all they are finding on these criminal kids is markers. You know you have to pull out the machine guns for maker toting dancing kids that "hug each other to much to be healthy".

Needless to say when we got to the ticket booth we were very relieved. We pay our fair and precede into the huge venue.

Its a classic music hall that seems to have been built in the early nineteen hundreds. It has a half crescent moon hallway that wraps around the back of the main hall and two ramps leading down to the main dance floor. The walls are chipped ornate sculptures of high society of the long distant pass. Gaudy naked Greek goddess held onto the roof tops with guarding eye of the events below. We walk down the sloping ramps to check out the main scene. The dance floor is packed with raving freaks of all kinds. Older, younger, black, white, spanish, asian all dancing together in complete peace and harmony. The lights are pulsing all around the sweating half naked bodies as screams of pleasure surge out every once in awhile from the thunderous sound. man I love this scene. The passion ,the all out abandon of the outside world to break free if not for just a few hours and truly feel our real selves. Clear our minds and bodies and get down to the very tribal ancient roots of our ancestors. Unity across all boundaries of life. Humans being just that. Human. Getting along in the celebration of life for the sake of living it.

The main stage is in the shape of a huge robot. Huge glowing eyes with smoke billowing out of its square block head. The Dj booth was located in the head of the robot. With Derek may already burning the decks. Jumping and screaming like a mad man. There were three decks set up and Derek was working all of them. Total showmanship. We need to find some acid and get with the fascination. Tena was always very good at finding acid ,compared to me. I was 6'3" 220 and looked very ominous to most little ravers. and they sure as hell would never sell me drugs. Tena was nineteen but looked 16 so they thought she was just like them. I guess it also helps she was so cute you wanted to eat her alive. She dipped to the back of the dance floor with me close behind. I sat down as she started to scan. She drifted a little off into the crowd as I watched the crazy scene laid out in front of me. Promoters selling there next great event that will be so much better than this one. Groups of little girls giggling with total fear in their eyes but braving through it like the soldiers they are. Liquid housers grooving in their own world of self imagined illusion.

Glow sticks going up into the air to land in the hands of a eager raver that would create a quick light show to dazzle the retina then toss it back up for the next twirling raver to catch. Tena quickly returned with a tall lanky hippy in tow. Dressed very low key but with long hair and that deep LSD smile that you get over the years of tripping the light fantastic. He seemed a little older but had very loving open eyes.

"You guys have to be careful out here, the man is everywhere. How much do you need?"

"10 please" Tena smirks his way.

"10,your not thinking about selling any in here are you?" looking very concerned now.

"No, No we would never do that, Im taking 5 and he is taking 5" Tena states firmly.

"5,this is really good acid are you sure you will be ok" as the look on the dealers face gets real concerned.

We give him a huge smile back and nod with confidence. He pulls out the strip and we tear it in half. We ate our portions right in front of him so there was no doubt where it was going. Right to our receptive little minds. and man as soon as it hit my tongue I knew we where in for it. It tasted like a silver metallic coin. Very strong. the dealer smiles and drifts of into the mass of freaks. Now its time for the fun!

Sitting in the back of the swarming masses the acid started to take hold of our minds. The ceilings were now a gliding mass of brilliant colors morphing and molding with the music. We looked at these events as much more than parties. They were a gate way to another universe. A universe of peace and friendship most normal people could not dream of. Dancing in complete ecstasy with our universal brothers and sisters. Cosmic unity throughout the universe. We started to dance. dance like the world was ending and that's all that is left to do. Dance. We slowly began to move into the mass of the dance floor. Starting at level one and working our energy up to move to the next level of the floor. Its almost like you have to have enough energy of spirit to get closer to the energy source. The speakers. The closer you get, the harder it gets to keep your composure.

The sonic waves of bliss wash over your soul renewing your whole spirit. Joy abounds from every limb, moving in ecstatic rhythm to the beat. We are now almost half way through the crowd, dancing through the sheets of freaks. Each energy level of the floor is watched and guarded by the gatekeepers. If your energy isn't right you will not pass the gatekeepers. These are usually big scary guys that you wouldn't want to pass if you had fear in your heart. Not us. We are cosmic and know all the gatekeepers needs. Your heart must be open and your soul must be free. You must dance like you are trying to get into god's lap. You must feel the universal love in every cell of your being. We dance harder and harder. The entrance into the front of the floor is opened by the final gatekeeper. The words "You can pass" are projected into our minds eye. getting closer now. almost there.

We were just a few rows back now from the stacks of speakers and we could see the stage very clearly now.

Derek was up there just killing the decks. Putting everything he had into moving this crowd. Fucking amazing. The music is at a roar now and the sonic waves wash over our souls. Everyone is moving in unison and the energy is so thick you can eat it with a spoon. The robot head is now huge in front of us and the place is going off. and our heads are in the fucking clouds baby. I look up at the staging area and notice a few dark figures gallivanting around next to the stage. they are looking down at the crowd pointing and laughing, apparently making fun of the lower forms of humans in the crowd. Then their appearance began to get more clear. They were very tall for humans and some had horns protruding from their now very demonic faces. These were the things that took enjoyment in fucking with human souls.

They would use any tactic they could to lower the energy level of a human. Anything they could do to stop humans from getting to a higher goal. and the fucked up part is that they are reflections of our own souls. All the fear, jealousy, hate, pain. These entities embodied this. The demons of the deep always show up if there are angels in the mist. We dance harder and harder. It feels as if we are departing from our physical selves and transcending into a state of pure soul. Not bound by skin. Getting higher and higher. No demon can bring us down. They are us and we are them. No denying what we are. We all have dark and light inside of us. It just matters which one you want to concentrate on.

We are now right in front of the main stack of speakers. The music is surging right into us. Rearranging our molecules, purifying our synapses. The music is one with all of us. It is us. It is coming from us. Straight from the crowd into the dj which places it back into the loop of creation to be re assimilated by our ears. Cosmic fucking unity. My eyes shift from the demons and look above them. I almost shit my pants.5 10 foot tall whitish Grey alien beings were looking down at the crowd. Scanning, processing, observing. I look around to see if I'm alone in noticing these huge aliens directing the show from above the stage. No one seems to mind or they already know what ive just witnessed. What am I talking about, these are the same beings from tunnel vision and family affair. What are they looking for. Are they watching over us like a scientist would observe their own mice in a laboratory. This is getting nuts. I'm sweating like I'm in the desert. We have been dancing straight for a good two hours now and I'm getting light headed as hell. Water. Oh yea forgot I still had a body. Still limited to skin. We head out through the masses to try and find some water.

Up the ramp and out into the hallway. and man oh man has that hallway changed in two hours. The walls were pulsing neon rainbow swirls rushing out onto the floor. Faces were melting and laughing and crying and yelling and kissing. All while melting. melting into each other. Almost seems as if the mass is its own and everyone is a limb of it. Everything mashes together in synced harmony of chaotic disorder. We swathe through the mass and see a vendor selling water by the fist full. No drinking fountain. Big money in selling water to dieing people.

"5 dollars" spouts the clerk as we shit ourselves over the cost. "per bottle" I questioned. "That's right how many do you want" he retorted. "2" a sheepishly waifed back. and then a few blissful soaking mouthfuls of god's one and true element, good old h2o.

It feels like my whole being is rejuvenated. I can feel the liquid fill into my body like filling an empty vase. Time to head back in. Its going to be a long journey.

"I feeeeel loveeeeeee, loveeeeeeeeeeeeee, loveeeeeeeee" comes pouring out of the main room to screams of ecstasy. We begin to descend down into the pit feeling very much like not having to go through what we just left. It was so intense that I don't know about repeating it tonight. Tena is feeling the same thing ,so we decide to leave. Mind you its been a little under 3 hours and we are still tripping like mad fiends. Oh well I've driving on acid before. We make our way past storm trooper central and out into the freezing fucking cold chi town air. Dam, I got so hot in there i took off my sweatshirt and now I have a t-shirt on. Fuck it, to far to go back. I'm tripping, the cold is only in my head. I make this my mantra while waiting for the Freddy Krueger bus to come and pick us up. The cops are giving crazy looks at the crowd outside since most of us only have t-shirts on now. They have full on winter gear and we are standing out here like its Florida. Dancing hard can really raise up that body temp. Up pulls the bus to cheers of delight. Oh so warm in the bus. Its not so scary now to. Now that we are leaving and everything seems ok, its quite inviting. Everyone is chatting and smiling. Even the bus driver seems to have loosened up over the evening.

Now he seems almost blissful.

We pull up to the parking lot as he exclaims "be careful driving kids" with the doors slipping shut behind his glowing smile.

Our car is covered in ice and takes some pushing and

pulling to get the doors open. We get inside the car and slam on the ignition. Its so fucking cold that there is ice on the inside of the car as well. We crank the heat and shiver. The windows are completely iced over. Got to scrape. The ice flies off the window with massive swirls of trails coming off every shard. Everything is still rainbow goo but I'm real comfortable with it now. When you get this high you don't think you are ever coming down. I jump back into the car with the wonderful feeling of heat pouring into my veins. The car is almost ready to go. and I'm still wondering how the hell I'm going to find the hotel now. The acid has completely destroyed all since of memory and or direction. Oh well guess the universe will get me there. Its got me this far.

We pull out into a transformed alien candy land. Everything is pulsing. The sky, the huge buildings, the sidewalks all mashing and molding in a beautiful symphony. The street lights are now huge bursting orbs of sunlight breaking into huge rainbows that rain the jelly down on the car. We pull up to a street light and notice a motorcycle pulling up. Riding this space machine was one of the other dimensional friends(alien life forms) giggling and waving. Their heads were full on rainbow grafting translucent liquid with the biggest smiles you have ever seen. They seemed very happy to see us and we had no idea what to do. As it pulls off in trails of liquid color they wave goodbye like long lost friends. What the fuck. Are we on another planet and didn't get the memo. Now all the vehicles we see are being drove by aliens, all smiling and laughing. Weird floating vehicles bubbling and shooting around with glee. Some are out in the air zooming off at lighting speeds.

I try to keep my composure and get us to the hotel. The city is melting down all around me.

The parades of aliens fly by as I'm wondering if we are dead. My skin is a shimmering sliver blue and everything in my visual field screams of the 4th dimension. I feel light as air and the car is floating around like it is a spaceship to. My hands feel like something else has grabbed hold and is guiding this whole ride. With astonishment we pull up at the hotel, run from the valet and make a dive for the lobby. The immaculate hotel is now a intricate temple of sorts. Huge pillars of stone rising into the infinite sky. The huge gothic murals were now alive and fully animated. The cherubs flying around with angelic hymns caressing the lobby ceiling. Gold slashing everywhere as we try to hold back our total amusement. Everything is now so dam hilarious that we cant even control the laughter. The whole scene has turned into a gothic comic book with the desk clerk towering into a 10 foot tall looming creature from mars. We shot by the Martian and take the ride up to our room. The hall ways are collapsing into pink cotton candy mud as we try to figure out the room number.

Once in the room a feeling of total safety washes over us. but only for a few seconds. I go to roll up a spliff and Tena has a very worried face.

"I just looked at myself in the mirror and I was an alien.

They were standing behind me showing me I'm one of them" she stutters.

I look in the mirror and sure as anything we were both aliens looking back from the glass. I waved and the helpers in the glass waved back as well. I jump from the mirror in total astonishment. Have we transformed over the night. Were we always one of them and we have taking on a human appearance. Needless to say my head was spinning. I went into the bathroom to try and shake it off .This was way to much. So I look like something from another planet. We are seeing these things and no humans. Maybe we are not supposed to be on this planet. Maybe there has been a mistake a universe control. Did we slip through the crack. Or maybe we are supposed to take matters into our own hands.

"We have to die. We cant be here anymore they want us to come home" i mumble thinking of how to kill myself without killing myself.

"We could strangle each other while we are making love, I've heard you can die from that" I suggest as Tena knods in agreement.

We both disrobe and start to kiss. Just the thought of dieing was so exhilarating we couldn't control the passion. We were now one and would die together, pass to the great unknown together. Our bodies molding into one sweaty mass of vibrating love. We began to grab each others necks and try this method of madness. We both found out real quick we couldn't grab each other hard enough to actually cut off the wind. Our bodies couldn't even register the request. So much for dieing like this. What to do. I know we are at the end of our lives and death is right around the corner. Where to go. How to get this done without breaking cosmic laws and pass through the gates. The thought entered my mind from out of no where.

"We are supposed to die in San Francisco, that's what we

are supposed to do. The golden gate bridge, that's where it will happen" I announced with great excitement.

We are going to San Francisco to die. That's where the story will end. The sun was beginning to break over the water of lake Michigan as began to pack for our journey. The acid was still running strong on our minds and we were ready for what destiny had prepared for us. We had heard the mission bell(well at least I did) and our exit was at hand. We paid our bill and set out to the car. We still had an once of herb with us and like 400 bucks. More than enough to get us to San Fran. No need for money when we get there because we are going there to die. The universe will take care of it. Just follow the yellow brick road to the water and that's it! Tena starts to roll up some joints and we head west out of Chicago. Nothing to stop us now. The day pushed on as i put the pedal to the metal. The acid must have been very very good because i was flying higher than a kite.

I hadn't slept in two days and had it dead set in my head I wasn't sleeping until I was at the golden gate bridge. I would put my head down in Tena's arms and die in my sleep. My mission was done and I was out of here for sure. All I had to do was get us there. No sleep. I flew through what i purpose to be Illinois and headed due west from there.

The next state i remember was Colorado. The sun was beginning to set and Tena was asleep. I had to stick to the mission. Get to San Francisco. I was trying to get down to the 40 not knowing San Fran was on the NORTH end of California. I figured it was only a couple hours north of Los Angeles being very wrong in my Midwest mentality of proportion. From the border of California to Los Angeles is 9 hours. You can drive the whole state of Ohio in 5. I was way off. The mountains of Colorado were covered in 7 foot snow drifts of undulating glop. It looked like going through a white tunnel with the very top chopped off. After going through the aspen pass, the snow disappeared and turned to sheer ice. I tried not to notice the "ride with spikes" signs and motored on to my destiny. The car would slide back in fourth in motion with the curves and lead the car closer and closer to the cliff faces every time. I stopped for the 4 dollar a gallon aspen gas and plowed through the evening snow. I was now leaving Colorado and the mountains and I was knocking on the west's door. The colors rise up from the pink hazy puffy licks of the early morning sun as the cascade of the flat plains is set out before me. The sunrise had never been so beautiful. The rays of the sun ran over the landscape of other worldly dimensions. I had never been west of St Louis and the terrain was totally new. Like being shot into a painting from some mythic artist from the future. Guiding every second with the precision of a master craftsman. Molding and shaping this interstellar show for our own spiritual growth. Showing me all of what earth has to offer in a single blow then I can leave mission accomplished. Only one more day to go. Then i can leave this crazy planet behind.

Chapter 7

Bay Bridge Breakdown

As we glided down the highway, mountains gave way to the open desert. Huge plateaus that you could imagine a tribe of native Americans charging down the cliffs to over take the pale face invader of their lands. We had completely run out of magic greens and were starting to feel the stress of reality seeping in. That wont do at all for these weary travelers. We are on the outskirts of Las Vegas at this point and all you can see is pawn shops on every street. Time to start selling of the rest of our things. I have a pager that would bring in a whole 8 dollars. Tena has a graduation ring that we pawn off for 30 bucks. That will get us enough gas to reach California. We have been asking everyone(not a good idea) if they can spare some weed for our tattered minds. Most just walk by with a look of complete disgust, some walk by and give you "I'm sorry for you but I'm just to busy in my own life to help you get high". Don't these people understand we are days away from our mortal death and all we need to do is get to San Francisco. And just a little weed would make it bearable to face. We keep moving down the highway which has loss all color to the light brown oceans of the California desert sands. We are getting so close now(not knowing we are heading straight to Los Angeles not anywhere near San Francisco).We are rolling up huge mountain overpasses and down freeways so immense it boggled the mind. It felt like we were driving up the side of the world. Huge 12 lane highways spread out as we came down the 5 freeway into the San Fernando basin. We need gas again. I pump ,Tena pays. I just finished pumping the last of the gas we had into the ride as Tena comes running out of the gas station with merry glee.

"This cool ass girl just gave me a huge bud and some rolling papers. She fully welcomes us to California and wishes us the best on our travels" Tena says with utter excitement.

I knew we were on the right path. Now onto San Francisco. Lets get directions here and head out. I ask a trucker walking by

"How far to San Fran" and he lets out a laugh from the depths of his belly.

"Go north about 300 miles and you'll be getting close" he smiles as we sit in total disbelief.

We just emptied the last money we had into the gas tank and that might get us 50 miles if that. Holy fuck. Now what (now I'm thinking of money problems right?). We sit and ponder for a few minutes while we puff on our charity bud we just picked up from the California greeting center.

Tena chimes in "I have a cousin at camp Pendleton that might lend us some money to get up to San Fran".

"Its not to far away from Los Angeles".

Sounds like a plan. Tena heads off to the pay phone. For two teenagers that had never been as far west as St Louis los angles might have well been another planet. Where else on earth would you find someone nice enough to help out two homeless tripping ravers with buds and papers. We were getting close to the goal. I could feel it coming like a freight train. Just a few more hours and we will be at our death. I will be back on my home planet in no time and we can leave this evil 3rd dimension behind us. Back to the world of beauty and freedom. Beyond skin. Beyond money, jobs, pain, death. Into the world of light. Only a few more hours. Tena gets a hold of her cousin and we head off to the military base he is stationed at. He doesn't have any money but said he can at least take us to dinner before we head off to San Francisco. We meet him at a Denny's and he was obliviously disturbed about seeing his cousin in such a condition. He was a clean cut down home kind of guy that had known Tena since she was child. We keep our plans to ourselves ,speaking around the fact of what has been going on back home. Or why we were out here driving around southern California with no money of any kind heading to San Francisco for who knows what.

Tena keeps the conversation small and quick and we don't eat much at all. We haven't ate in days and when you get that far into starvation eating actually hurts. No need for food. We had evolved beyond food and were knocking on heavens gates. We say our quick goodbyes and head down the road. We have a full tank of gas and 300 miles to go before SF. May the stars be with us to guide us home. I drive through the night heading up the 5 North with a vengeance. The sun is just pulling up over the rolling grasslands of Northern California. the sun burning through the last of the evening fog and we are now totally out of gas and money for real this time. Nothing left to pawn and no one to turn to. We pull into a BP gas station as the car sputters to a halt. I notice a little book bus on the other side of the pump with a hippie looking middle age man pumping gas into the vehicle. We look pretty tattered at this point having not showered, slept or ate in three days, so I'm sure we were a sight to behold. Tena gets out and heads right up to the man.

"I hate to bother you sir but we are lost heading to San Francisco. We were wondering if you could help us out with gas money" she whimpered in a defeated tone.

We had hit rock bottom and were now homeless people asking for gas money at gas station. Oh how the tides can turn on you in just a few days and end up in this situation. We were both from good homes and decent families. I just dropped out of school not two months ago and now my girlfriend is begging for gas money. No time for thinking must keep going. This is how it goes before you die. You lose everything and you face it alone with nothing. Keep moving don't think. The very warm decent hippie fellow was a traveling children's book salesman and was like an angel from above.

"I wont give you money but ill fill up your tank. I wouldn't feel right flat out giving you money" he said in "that" tone.

The tone of "I don't want to support your drug habit and be responsible for killing you". Well in fair, its nice enough to have gas to reach our final destination.

"Thank you so much for your help" we both say in unison.

" Your very welcome, be careful out here on the road, it can be very dangerous. Not everyone out here is so nice" as he waves leaving us behind in a cloud of dust.

The first sight of San Francisco might as well been OZ. Pulling across the first major bridge is something that can take your breathe away at first sight. The huge pillar skyscrapers surrounded by oceans on all sides. The buildings caressed by the whisking clouds of the bay. The sun gleaming through in rays that look like a slide up to heaven. We have made it. The place of our death and release into paradise. We follow the main freeway over the ocean. Tena guides us through the hills like she was born here. We are now drifting on idle because we have no gas. So she puts it in neutral and rolls down the hills to get enough momentum to make it back up the next hill. We are totally lost. We got stopped at a street light and look onto the center curb.

There is a homeless man with rags draped over his body covered in layers of dirt. His eyes are wild in fascination and he is holding a scale of some sort. It looks like a judgment scale. He is screaming to the heavens in some guttural moan of agony. All the while with a smile on his face. Holy shit. We start to roll again and this time we are back onto a little freeway and the car is jerking bad. We have to pull over now. It's the end of the road.

Tena makes a quick turn to the right and follows a little access road. She pulls into a parking space as the car dies. She tries to start it and gets denied. Nothing. she is out of gas. We gaze out in front of us in amazement. We have landed at the golden gate bridge parking lot. Laid out before us is one of the most famous bridges in history. Seagulls soaring over head welcoming us. The sun boar down in its glorious blaze. This is it. This is the place we die. Well we are here and we are not dead. Must be tonight. All we have to do is wait for sleep tonight and we will wake up in paradise. We walk down and get what we think is our one and last glimpse of the pacific ocean. When you think your mortal end is near everything is amazing. Every detail is registered on a different scale. The fisherman look like Norman Rockwell paintings encompassing the passion and right in humanity. A sea lion comes up to us as we are sitting on the dock. It seems to be communicating to us. As if the lion knew we were coming to a higher state and wanted to welcome us. It could feel our cosmic love uniting with the creator and wanted to acknowledge our quest. All the signs are there. There was a feeling of wholeness in the air. A feeling of overwhelming relief and happiness.

Could this be the night I can leave this nightmare behind. As we sit on the dock looking over the bay, Tena and I hold each other tighter and tighter. .The sun is setting and we are ready for our end. Our love for each other has grown over the past weeks. We have rarely left each others side for more than a few minutes. It feels as if we have lived lifetimes in the past weeks. Getting to know each other on levels most humans will never be able to understand. The true feeling of knowing all you have is each other and nothing else matters. Its been a long journey and we are both exhausted beyond imagination. No food, sleep, money, family or friends. Out in the perimeter, as they say. We make our way to back our car and notice a bright orange ticket on the windshield. I guess you have to put money in those meters. Whoops. No matter death comes. We wont be here in the morning. We nestle in and lay down for our final sleep.

"I love you Tena" I whisper into her ear. "I love you to, lets get some sleep" she murmurs back drifting to sleep.

Total exhaustion washes over my whole being. Good bye cruel world. I hear noises all around. Laughs and giggles coming from all around the car. Are they here. I cant fight off the sleep as the giggles seep into the distance.

Into the deep black. We awake to first light. I leap up expecting only the best. Nope. Still here. Same parking lot surrounded by tourists. Good god we are in hell. Clamoring tourists of all shapes and sizes in every direction. Looking into the car laughing and joking at the sight of the two homeless people. We are not dead in any form. But we are dead SOBER. Starving from real hunger and dead SOBER. There are now multiple tickets on our hood and reality is kicking in hardcore folks. Everyone around us is on vacation, clean cut, eating ice cream and running around giggling. Giggling and laughing with all the amusement in the world. We hadn't showered in 5 days and just came from the alien city of tripperdom. Holy crap how are we getting out of this.

There is no paradise, no death. Just more life in the worst situation possible. We just left Columbus owing the very wrong people 30,000,have no money, more importantly no drugs and no way home. And starving like you cant believe. When the drugs wear off that evolved level of existence turns on you quick. Now trash was looking very, very , very good. that's right folks. Trash. We started to beg. From everyone we could. Most scoffed and most looked the other way without even a word.

Mostly it was: "get a job" "get out of the way"

and of course the younger crowds pure laughter of enjoyment. Now the trash was the only option. I waited until someone threw a half eaten hot dog in and I grabbed it. Tena refused as I ate without even thinking twice. I almost threw it back up out of total disgust of myself but my body held it in like it was the last supper. Despair began to set in and all hope was gone. I had gone completely mad out of my skin and lead the love of my life on a death trip. As the sun set on this day the golden gate bridge did not shimmer in glory. It loomed as the place hundreds of lost desperate souls had thrown themselves off of into the pacific ocean. It echoed as the sign to me that suicide must be the only option at this point. I will take matters into my own hands this night and end this thing once and for all. The night chill had set in and I told Tena of my plan. I was going off the golden gate bridge. Tena began to weep.

"Please this is not it, we have to go back and face this. It will be ok. I promise this is not the answer."

I began to get furious.

"This cant be my life. How did this happen. In a matter of a few weeks. It went from parties and space and friends and growth. Now its drug dealers, killers, cops, starvation, pain, death. There cant be a god that lets this happen. I have to see for myself. I walked through the garden holding gods hand. Danced through the kingdom of light and laughed with the angels. I don't want life. I want to be with god. Out of this hell".

Tena cries even harder.

"Call your mom, tell her what your doing, call your mom". Tena pulls on my arm and drags me to a pay phone under the bridge.

I thought it might be a good idea to tell my mom good bye. and it turns out it was. and wasn't. "hello" , my mom answers the phone already in tears.

"Where have you been" she hammers "Mickey p has

been over here. What the hell have you got yourselves into. You owe him how much. he said there are tags on your heads. they are looking to kill both of you. Get the hell back here right now and make this right."

"I'm going to jump off this fucking bridge that's it mom, do you want to hear as I jump from this fucking thing. I'm sorry"

Now I'm crying and screaming as well. "I'll fucking do it Ill jump with you here on the phone". She bolts back in hysterics

"Why would you do this to me and your father, calm down and listen to me. what is it going to take for you to get back here. Mickey P is saying if you at least meet with him that things can be worked out. They don't want it to come to something more, but if you keep hiding it looks like you did it. Just come back and talk with him. what do you need to get home."

"I need money, we have nothing, no gas and our car is going to get towed. We need help now momma, please help us" now I'm crying and begging.

Desperation will make you go to levels you cant even begin to imagine. Turns out my mom has a close friend in Oakland and will be out in the morning to help us. He is a doctor. I've known him for a little bit. My mom used to baby sit for their child. Very nice guy that I did not even know moved out here.

"Just hang on until the morning and help will be there" pleaded my now mentally ravaged mother.

"I'm sorry I will make this right, we just need to get home.

Thank you so much mom, I will call you in the morning. Tell him we are in the golden gate parking lot. Thank you so much." as I sigh a breath of some relief for the first time in a long time.

Even though there are drug dealers out to kill me. Out of the frying pan into the fire. Tena looks totally defeated and ready to go home now. And I don't blame her one bit. We look and smell like death. Hunger is constant pain and suffering. It never ends. We walk back to the car feeling reality soaking into every bone. What the hell is Mickey p going to do. he could just have us killed as we are showing up. this is so bad but it must be done. Who knows what the hell they will do.

They might go after our families next. Then what. We have to go back and face this head on. I was just chasing what I thought was death down like an amusement, all the while masking the truth of facing death at the hands of these dealers. No where to go but back home. There is no way this is going to be good. We were awoke by tapping on the glass of the car.

The sun was fully up and shining and all the tourist were back in full swing. My mom's friend was tapping at the glass. His name was Jeff. Medium built guy with a very nice demeanor and was polite as he good be. Needless to say I was completely embarrassed to see him at this point. How do I explain to this guy we were contacted by aliens who I thought telepathically told me to go to San Francisco and die at the golden gate bridge. He didn't ask any questions, it was all over our faces.

"I'm going to take you guys over to a hotel so you can get cleaned up. Ill fill your tank up and get you some food to. You guys don't look like you've ate in awhile right?".

Just the talk of food made us crawl out of our skin.

"oh yes please food sounds very good" me and Tena chime in like school children.

He pulls out a gas can out of his trunk and fills up the car. The feeling of thanks and remorse over our actions sinks in. He doesn't really look at me which gives me a horrible feeling of shame. I'm a grown guy and now one of my old family friends has to come out and give me food, shelter and money. How fucking embarrassing does it really get. He fills up the car with gas and we head out of the city. We drive over a bridge and pull into a suburb of Oakland. Tena and I haven't really spoke much and I'm sure she is feeling the brunt of pretty much no sleep or food for over a week now. We pull into a motel and our friend goes up to get a room for us for the night. He comes back out and comes over to the car.

"There is a shopping mart right over there. I'll run over there and get you guys some groceries. and then you can shower up".

We smile and say thank you over and over. Thank God for this individual. I don't know what would have happened to us if we didn't get any help. He comes back with bags of food and walks us up to the room. It's a small little room with beautiful little flowers every where. It smelled and looked like heaven itself. We say our goodbyes to our new found savior and he graciously shuts the door behind him. We turn around and get the first real look of ourselves in weeks. We both just sit in awe of how we looked.

We had been in the same clothes now for a week and hadn't showered in the same time. We were covered head to toe in layers of dirt and nastiness. Our hair was matted with dirt and sweat. Our faces were covered with dirt , so you couldn't really see our skin at all. What a fine mess this is. We both head directly to the shower. I cant describe the feeling of that water washing off the dirt. More than bliss. The layers of dirt wash down the drain as we embrace under the cleansing water. We hadn't touched each other bodies in a while and hers felt like butter through my fingers. I feel the agonizing feeling of complete failure. I had just totally lost my mind and lead her down a path of sheer destruction. And didn't even look back or question what was going on. I have been the fool my dear sir, I have been the fool. Our clothes need sand blasted but we will be home soon, so we will get by stinking for a couple more days. We snack on the groceries but its still hard to eat to much after our stomachs had shrank so much. Pretty much all we can really think about at this point is sleep. Oh beautiful sleep. On a actual bed. Oh glory be to a soft mattress and pillows. The little things you take for granted sometimes. The fragile little things that are so precious when stripped away. I wrap my arms around Tena who is already heading to sleep. I slightly kiss her ear and whisper "I love you sweetheart" as I drift to dreamland myself. We awake to the morning sun and don't want to leave our little paradise. Hotel rooms can do that to you. You think its permanent sometimes. Like this is really your house of luxury and the whole world doesn't exist. Our new found friend left us with gas money and its time start the journey home. We slide our crusted clothes back on and head out to the car. Its one of those beautiful pre spring days in San Francisco. Huge blue sky with birds flying everywhere. The looming fact of what we are going back to is sinking into the pit of my stomach. What's going to happen when we go back? What the fuck happened with Andres? Did he steal our shit or did he really get popped? So many questions start to race through my sober mind. What the fuck is Mickey P going to do to us. Is he going to believe a word we say or is it going to be lights out stage left. Doesn't matter now it's the only way to make things right. I cant believe he would threaten my family. Holy shit has this all got totally out of control. Why is this all happening. Why am I on this fucked up planet with these people. I cant even remember what planet I came from. I know I didn't want to land in a place like this. I place of pain, agony, starvation, crime, punishment, gravity, skin, money. This is what hell is. But everyone seems ok with it. Like we are the ones with the problems. Well dear sir I have some problems oh yes I do. With this world. This planet. This species of destruction. My mission has to be close to over. I cant be stuck on this place for what this species calls a "lifetime". Oh my God what if that's the case. What if I cant go back to my planet. What if I'm stuck here. Oh creator of the universe tell me it isn't so. We find the route 66 E road sign and head east on the legendary highway of death toward our destiny. The questions will be answered soon. Very soon.

Chapter 8

Innocent Laughter

We head back into Columbus with our lives a stake. We have a death tag on both our heads. We owe a killer gangster at least 30,000. They know where our parents live. We have no choice but to face Mikey p and hope for the best. At least our families will be safe and it will all be over. The least that could happen is that we both end up dead. And that doesn't sound like that bad of an option at this point in the game. We need to call him and set up a meeting point that will work in our favor. Totally public. Police close by. Easy in and out. Maybe if we can just see it coming we will be able to hit the gas and get away. No way of telling what's going to happen now. How did it all come to this. We were just partying. Having fun. Having the time of our lives we thought. Now we face our mortal death over money. One night deciding our fate forever. How fragile life is. Just one slip and its lights out.

"Hey Mickey, yea its me" Tena shyly states into the phone.

"Where the fuck have you guys been, why the fuck didn't you call me" I can hear Mickey screaming like a madman on the other end of the phone.

We are fucked. Royal fuck.

"Shit went real bad and I panicked, they said he got busted and the cops were coming. I freaked out and ran. I didn't know what the fuck to do, I didn't know if they had you or what the fuck went down. So I ran Mickey, fucking ran" tears now streaming down Tena's face.

"I thought I was doing the right thing. I thought the phones were bugged and the whole fucking thing flew out of control. What was I supposed to do".

Tena wipes away the tears as the voice on the other end has quieted down. I can't make out what is being said but Tena's tears have stopped and now the worry is back across her face. She puts down the phone without a word and looks at me in a way I will never forget the rest of my life.

"He wants us to meet him in an hour. He wants to ask us face to face what really happened. This could be it. I think he is going to kill us" as the tears well down Tena's face like a river.

These are real tears and I have no idea what the fuck to do. Should we run. Then our parents are surely dead. A level of fear and impending doom crawls at my skin. There is no way out but to face this. Face our deaths. We hold each other hard. Real hard. When you think you have minutes to live everything changes. Everything is slowed down. Like your mind naturally knows that death is upon you. Things come into focus. The things you'll miss. The things you didn't do. The people you didn't get to say goodbye to. The urge deep down in your bones to run but knowing there is no hope of getting away. My time here is almost up. This thing called life on this planet for this species is nothing but pain. Suffering. Cruelty. Confusion. Corruption. Why would anyone want to live here anyway.

The meeting is set up for a golf course in a little suburb of the city. Very open. Police station near by. Looks like Mickey p had the same idea. I don't know if that's I good thing or a bad thing. We pull into the access road to get to the parking lot as a fully tinted truck pulls in close behind us. Holy fuck we are now being followed. Is it Mickey's guys or the fucking cops. Panic rolls down our spines like waves of needles washing over your skin.

The truck keeps rolling as we pull into the parking lot. Mickey is parked with his front out. Looks like he is just as nervous as us about this whole thing. Holy God please get us through this mess. We really need you right now.

Mickey waves for us to get into the car. He is in the front and wants us in the back.

"Come on and don't look so dam nervous, your making us look shady as hell" Mickey assures us as we expect him to shoot us on the spot.

"You guys had us really pissed, I had to put out tags on you. You just disappeared. No word. No phone call. Nothing. One day you are here. The next your gone with everything. What would you have thought if this happened to you." Mickey states surprisingly calmly with no real anger in his voice.

"So needless to say when it came across the news that the cops had nabbed your boy Sam in mexico for fleeing during an investigation it started to all make sense. Did you know he was setting you up? You guys are real lucky he didn't just turn you over."

What the fuck is Mickey talking about? It turns out Sam was narcing us out. He had been busted months before on a growing op charge and was looking to set up Tena all along. The weight we gave to him that night was our bust. Instead of turning in Tena, he took the weight and

106

left town hoping to use the money to get away. Sam actually ended up saving all our asses. Even Mickey P.

"Everything has been evened up. You guys are going to have to pay this back some way but for now we are even. There are no more tags and no one will bother you. Forget you know my name" as he waves us out the door of the car.

Tena and I get out of the car with the swiftness of the angels wings that just pulled our souls from the abyss. A new lease on life. The overwhelming feeling of total exhilaration. We are going to live. Mickey P knew it. He knew that if the bust went down he would have been next on the pole. He would have been going down with us. He wanted so bad to kill us but if anything happened to us then it would put him right in the cross hairs of the cops. He knew that there was nothing left to do but cut his losses and let it go. We pull out of the parking lot with total glee. We need to celebrate and celebrate hard. Tena stops at a pay phone and dials the number.

"Hey Cregg, we are coming by to pick up some L, be there soon".

Cregg was some low level dealer scum bag type that would buy from us here and there. Turns out he had some for a change and it was supposed to be the bomb L drop. Yea I know. I know. After all that we still need some more trip. You would think after getting away alive with all the prior activities we needed to tempt fate just one more time. Just one more for the road bar keep. Just for old time sakes. Jesus. No logic at all. Just one more trip to the homeland and I will be satisfied with this boring thing called life. If I must. If I must follow the law of the land then so be it. It does not look like my ticket home is coming anytime soon, so I better deal with it. Gravity never felt so heavy.

Cregg lives in a shitty dump on the east side of town and we are getting to feel right at home in these dark places of earth. The places where light never shines and the shadows crawl with a greedy smile. Waiting for the next hapless victim to slip into their slimy grasps. How many times have we slipped through your devilish fingers. Cregg opens the door with a fiendish grin and slams the door behind us. " How goes it weary travelers of the night" he seethes out of his rotted mouthed. Cregg is the usual white trash. Greasy orange mullet slicking down the back of an acne ridden neck. His apartment smells of trash and urine. The paint flicks off the water damaged walls. The furniture droops to the floor while the carpet has morphed into its own color of rusty brown and yellow spots. He follow him into his roach infested kitchen hoping to get this over quickly and be on our way.

"I haven't seen you guys in a while" as Cregg tries to hug Tena in the nastiest way a man could possible try to hug a woman.

"Yea its been a long time" as Tena slips by him and I grab his hand crushing the bones in his slimy fingers. "Yea, yea" shaking the blood back into his fingers.

"This L is supposed to be out there, its called the bald eagle" as Cregg pulls out a book of crisp clean perfed paper of bliss.

"You guys should be able to handle it though, your master trippers right" Cregg the slime ball smirks.

"Lets just get to it, we really have to get ready for this party tonight." I state firmly as the walls of this shit whole start to close in on me.

There is a small rave tonight in downtown Columbus and we figured it would be fun to get out of my mom's house for the night. That's right. Even after all the hell I have put them through, my mom & dad are letting us stay in my old room.

I hate coming to these places. These dens of evil and corruption. People that seem to have the molecule we need for travel are these low life "sub human" beings. They have no respect for the drug. They think its fun "to get fucked up" and sit around all night giggling at the mirror. Never traveled to the higher planes. Never faced their true selves for the good and the bad. Tripping is not fun. It is scary. That's part of the trip. Its like life. You never know what's gong to happen but it is usually ok in the end. Most of the time. At least that's my small experience in the last few months in this human body. These people no nothing about what this stuff can really do. It changes worlds. Changes people. Changes nations. This is why the powers that be hate it the most. Out of all the drugs that exist for a human to take, this one little molecule causes fear like no other substance on earth. With one a drop a person may be freed from life times of repressed feelings and pain. To be released from the weight of the world for just a few hours and feel the world like a child. This was the power of LSD. The paper had little eagles with lighten bolts in their mouths.

Very strange artwork for acid.

"Yea yea its brand new, I haven't seen anything like it

before" Cregg boasts proudly over the paper he knew we adored.

"We will take ten" I plainly whiff his way as Cregg begins to ruffle his brow.

"What, I thought you guys were players" getting more miffed by the second.

"I have all this and all you want is ten, why don't you take more, its fine Ill front it out to you".

Man he sure is being friendly and its making us nervous as hell. Cregg never fronts out anything ever and now he is ready to drop this new L on us and wants to front out.

"No, no actually we are just really, really broke and cant handle any weight, sorry just cant do it right now.

"Aww man, are you sure come on you can take more, I'm sure you got some buddies or something that will take them off your hands".

Now Im getting freaked out. Is Cregg fucking setting us up to.

"Man, should I check you for a wire or something" as I pull at Cregg's shirt real quick to take a look.

"No, no I just need to get rid of it, I thought you guys would want more so I over did it, its my bad"

Cregg the snake shifts back and pulls his shirt out of my hand. "10 it is, let me go get the scissors real quick".

See what I mean. Just to get ten hits some from some low level asshole is a fucking hassle. A scam. A hustle. I guess everyone has to eat and that's why I hate this planet more and more everyday I have to be grounded in this god awful dimension of the human race. I want to go back to my home planet so bad it hurts to even think of it now. Just the thought of the roads of liquid gold make me breakdown in every cell of this body. I just don't think about it and adapt.

Overcome and survive. Good god what have I become. Cregg snips off our tickets and we leave with little good byes. Creggs not that bad of a guy. Just a product of the environment he has grown up in. Cant blame him. Its just the way it is. No matter. We have our fuel for the evening. Its off to another rave and another chance to leave this planet behind. Even if its only for a few, small precious hours.

We need to stop back by my mom's house to get ready for the evening and get directions. The plan was to take the acid at my mom's house, take a nap, and wake up tripping. Then we would head off to the rave tripping before we showed up at the show. That's right. We actually planned this. This was what we thought we be a great idea. Drive through the town peaking on acid looking for an underground illegal party so we could dance to the break of dawn. This was the raver way. Or it was at least our way. To test our minds under the most extreme situations. To push the boundaries of reality as far as they could be pushed and then push some more. The acid test of the twenty first century would be released out onto the streets. The test would be to survive in the beast that had been created by industrial society. To be able to dream where dreams never live. To use the tools of our ancestors to connect to the life line of love that flows from all existence. Yes we were out of our minds. But someone had to do the job.

and we took our position very seriously.

My parents were already asleep by the time we got home, so we slipped in nice and quiet. No need to awake my poor parents. Oh the trials I have put them through over the past year. Dropping out of college, disappearing with Tena, selling drugs, taking huge amounts of drugs, having people threaten their lives over my dumb ass mistakes, acting like I was going to jump off the golden gate bridge and so on. They don't deserve what I do. They were good parents. I guess. I cant remember much before the tunnel. Its all fuzzy and confused.

But they seem to love me even after all these things I have done. That's what love must mean. Even after causing so much pain to let me back into their home with no questions asked. We head upstairs to my bedroom and change our clothes. Tena really is a beautiful girl.

So little and fragile but underneath a solider at arms. She has made it through situations that would make most men lose their minds.

Under any condition she is ready to pull through. My love for her has grown to overwhelming proportions. We have spent every second together since new york. We haven't left each other sides. It feels like we are no longer individuals but a unit that has been molded together synthetically.

We are sitting in the dark on my bed laying side by side. I don't know why I thought doing acid in the dark with Tena was a good idea again after the mountain experience but here we are again in the dark on 5 hits of acid. This time with my parents not a few feet away in the next bedroom.

Actually from the sounds of it dad has falling asleep on the toilet again and is snoring loud enough to wake the gods. Only been about fifteen minutes had gone by when I here the giggle monster start with Tena.

"Teee heeheee" its starts softly but is now getting louder and louder. "Come on honey my parents are right in the next room" I start to plead

to the giggles coming from under the covers. " Tee ha HA HA HA HA HA HA" she blares out.

101 "I cant control it its just so funny, I cant stop laughing"

Tena is now in the middle of the room holding her hand over her mouth laughing to the point of tears. And I'm ready to lose my mind.

"I'm gonna pee myself ,I have to get into the bathroom" holding her private area with one hand and her mouth with the other as tears pore down her face.

"I don't know what to tell you, my dad is in the bathroom up here and my brother is in the downstairs bathroom. Your going to have to hold it. Please calm down. We will get out of here soon".

Tena is half jumping up and down and squiggling while laughing and crying at the same time.

"I'm going to have to go I cant hold it any longer" while she is removing her pants to the ankle position and squatting to pee.

And away we go. Tena is full on laughing hysterically as she is pouring a puddle onto my bedroom floor.

"That's it we have to get out of here or the shit is going to hit the fan" grabbing up Tena's pants and dragging her still laughing body downstairs heading straight for the car.

Mind you we are now 40 minutes into a 5 hit acid trip and I'm about to start driving down the road looking for a party in the middle of the city. This is not going to go anywhere good quick.

Chapter 9

Into the Darkness

I pull Tena in the car as I stop and get my bearings. The acid is coming on but I can handle it so far. Tena always gets it first though because she is so much smaller than me. She is totally out of it. Laughing like a mad woman. I guess we are headed for one hell of a ride. The car is almost transparent at this point, almost like the frame is there but everything else is made of see through plastic. I can see the road under my feet but I can still kinda make out the controls. I heard the party was downtown so I head west up past the airport into the main freeway heading north into the city. We are blasting Hardfloor's "strawberry fields" as the hallucinations come in like tsunami bowls of rainbow jelly. I am driving down the freeway as the light poles bend over our heads then snap back with delightful glee. The freeway has broken up into dozen of optional freeways as I have learned to always pick the one in the middle. The concrete flows in kaleidoscope swirls of elaborate swishing fluid, washing this way and that way as we putter off into the gem filled space station. Tena is in a completely different world.

"They are mind fucking me" Tena moans rubbing her body down past the border.

Who the fuck is they.

"Oh yea, Ohhhhh" as Tena is getting mind gang banged by the phantom mind fuckers.

Panic rips through me. I see a car next to us on the freeway and must be those people who are fucking my girlfriends mind. I must put a stop to this right now. I must stop these phantom mind fuckers from rapping my girlfriends mind. I slam the brakes and head for the next exit. The mindfuckers are following now.

They are exiting to, they want Tena. They are coming for her. I jet down the off ramp ,cut into an alley, all the while the mindfuckers are in close pursuit. Now there are three cars. Where the fuck are these things coming from. I pull down another side street and head into a dead end. The Mfers are right beside us now and its coming to a head. I blast the brakes, slam it into reverse and swipe around the front end of the car. I hit the gas and leave the phantoms in the dust. What the fuck. I look into the rear view mirror and there is nothing there. I swear to god, not one car. nothing.

Where the fuck am I. Where the fuck is the freeway and how the hell did I get into this alley. Tena is staring off into outer space, very quiet now and acts as if nothing had just happened. Did I make all that up. What the hell was I thinking. Or was I thinking. Or did that really happen, my mind spinning out of total control. Must keep moving. Must keep driving. The road is a smear of multi layered play dough. Nothing is solid. Nothing is static. Everything sways to the motion of my mind. I am in control of the fantasy world.

I am the master of this universe. My ego is now playing tricks on me. Its that feeling you get when you feel as if you've been let in on a big secret. How to control your own brain and make it control your physical reality. Mind over matter. In its truest sense of the word. That this molecule can let you use your brain in ways you never could before imagine. I am now controlling all the street lights to go green as they all flash green all the way down the road. This power should not be played with. Its like being a child all over again and having your superpowers actually work. When your pillow case turns into a real cape and you go flying into the air.

But even being superman I couldn't figure where the hell this party was to save my life. Two hours has gone by and it feels like a year. Pissing, folding freeways, falling light posts, mind control over reality. What could possible be next at this party. If we can ever find it. I pull out onto another freeway and hope for the best.

Tena has calmed down a bit and has been pretty quiet since the mind fuck. The freeway is now a 2 lane highway and its getting darker by the second. Dam it we must be heading away from town and not to it. I pull over into a parking lot to try and figure out where the hell we are. Everything is out of proportion when your tripping real hard. It all seems like the end of the world sometimes. Logic just isn't logical at this point in the game. I flip on the light and the car is filled with chaos. The dashboard breaks up into geometric shards of plastic dripping down the panels onto the floor. I don't know where we are at all.

Totally lost out in the dam boondocks and have no idea how the fuck we got here. Tena just stares back with total despair and a horrible lost look in her eyes. The look makes me panic and start to lose it. Oh shit what have I done. We are in for it. What do we do. Blam!!! As huge white blinding lights burn behind us. One of the lights is moving and coming at us. There is a voice attached to it.

"Hey there" the sheriff politely asks from the stream of his light saber. "Yes sir, were we doing something wrong?" I peer back through the blinding rays.

"Well you guys are sitting out here in the middle of this parking lot and we were just checking to make sure you were doing ok".

"Its pretty late out here and you guys looked real young so we usually stop when there is a chance you could be under age".

Dam. Tena and her young ass looks. She still gets carded for 18 and over movies because she looks so young. Cops probably thought we were out here fucked up and up to no good. Oh that's right we are.

"Well lets see your ids, if your clean you'll be on your way".

The sheriffs way of telling us to get moving without telling us to get moving. Slick words for sure. We hand over the ids as I start the usual what the fuck did I leave out and forget. The hideaway bong is in plain site, Tena has L in her purse(or did we eat it all, I cant remember), and our pupils are ripped open. Well this could be it.

"Here you go, everything checks out, be on your way now" the officer states swiftly.

We don't even get a chance to see him get into his car and pull away. And off he goes blasting down the long dark road. We both look at each other in complete disbelief. Did that really happen. by the looks of our faces it sure seemed to happen to both of us. Holy crap what the fuck is going on. Now what do we do. We still don't know where the fuck we are at. Tena looks like she is getting ready to break down and cry. I guess we keep driving and hope to see something or find someone that can get us back to town. Please something out there just get us home. The road isn't getting any brighter and we haven't seen another car forever. Did we finally enter some alternate reality. Did we make the jump. This isn't the world of light and love I remember. This place is dark as the void. Our headlamps barley pierce the night while we sputter down the highway. Sputter. Sputter is not good. Ub Ub Ub Ub errrrrrrrrrrrrrrrrrrrrrr. I look down in total dam shock. We are totally and completely out of gasoline. This can not be happening. Not now.

"What's going on" Tena whimpers in a shy worn out tone. "It's the gas, we are on E" slapping my head down on the wheel. "I guess we have to start walking and try and get some gas" "Where?". "I have no clue but we have no choice".

We both drag our fully wasted minds out onto the road and start heading off into the darkness. We just leave the car in the middle of the road and start walking. No idea where but we just started walking. From the looks of the ragged fence and lack of street lights I would say we are in the country somewhere. There is no moon out and the sky is black satin. There looks like a building of some sort coming up but it looks pretty dark. As we came up on the building it took the form of an old abandoned church. And holy shit did the place look evil as evil could get. You could almost hear screams of agony coming from inside. This church was not inviting. It scared the shit out of Tena and I. Straight to the bone. And just as we passed the church a huge glowing orange vehicle pulled right up behind us blazing its emergency lights.

"Hey you guys, is that your car up the road?" screamed a very burly roadside worker.

"What the hell is the matter with you, get the hell out of the middle of the street" rushing towards us looking very, very upset.

"Get into the truck, why did you just park your car in the middle of the road. This is a heavy trucker road and your lucky one didn't just run you both over"'.

"We ran out of gas sir" I whimper like a wounded dog. "Well lets go get some quick before you don't have a car to come back to".

He slams the gas pedal as we rip down the road. I can see lights up ahead that looks like a gas station. We were only maybe 2 miles away. 2 miles and we would have seen civilization. Man acid plays tricks on your mind like no other chemical on earth. The angelic road worker stops at the station and fills up his reserve tank. Its amazing the people who come into your life so randomly at the perfect time. He could have been anyone and just went by us. As a matter of fact people did just drive by us. Two people walking down the middle of the road in the middle of the night. The worker jumps back in his truck quickly as we try to hold our ravaged minds together. We get smart for two seconds and ask the driver if he knows the address we started our journey off to find to begin with.

"Why would you want to go to that part of town" as the driver raises an eyebrow of suspicion for the first time at his two broken down travelers.

"That's a real dangerous side of town but Ill write down the directions for you anyways" pulling out a marker and piece of paper from his pocket.

The elaborate design he drew looked alien in origin. With every swoop of the pen new flowing patterns would erupt from the page.

"You got it" looking at me for some type of acceptance I guess. "Sure no problem" I replied as we jumped out to pour the gas into our car.

"Hurry up, wait a second let me do it" as the driver jumps out of the vehicle.

"Some one could be coming any time" as the driver splashes gas all over from his frightened hands, shaking hands.

"Get in and see if it starts" he barks jumping back into his truck. I jump in and it starts right up. Thank god. This guy just saved our

lives for sure. "Thank you so much" I yell out to the driver who is already flying away with lights growing dimmer in the distance.

Well here we are in the middle of nowhere with a alien map to a party that might not be a good idea to head to, even if we can find it. And we are both on 5 hits of acid complexly tore up out of our minds. Tena in barley hanging on by a thread and I cant say that I'm any better. I hit the gas and make a u turn towards the direction the truck took off to. Just as we swing into the other side of the road a massive roar zooms by our car. A huge semi truck barreling down the freeway going a easy 60 mph.

"The world is falling apart, we are destroying the world" Tena begins to mutter.

And as if on cue I start to see the trees start to wither and crumble.

"We are destroying the world stop it stop it" Tena now screams at the top of her lungs.

She is becoming frantic and I have some how been pulled into her hallucination. The trees are falling. The road begins to crumble in front of the car. And I mean literally it looked as if the road was falling apart under the car.

"We are destroying the world, I can feel all the pain, it is coming through me" Tena sobs through rivers of tears.

She is now pulsing back and forth while I am watching the road crumble in the rear view mirror. The world is falling apart. Our world. Their world. Were we looking into the future of the earth. When all the material world would disintegrate. When we would watch the whole world crumble right in front of our eyes.

"Please stop, I have to get it out of me please stop somewhere" she pleads while I look for another gas station stop at.

We must have traveled a lot farther then I thought because the gas our friend gave us is now almost gone again. And the sun is peaking through the massive wasteland the world has become in our reality. Burned trees, dead grass, buzzards chopping at rotted flesh. This is the world of the dead. How did this happen overnight. We left town tripping our faces off and now we return to a burnt husk. How much time has gone by. Years. Decades. We were moving across the boundaries of time to witness what would become real one day soon. The waves of fear and horror cannot be written on the page properly. Life extinguished. And we get to live with it.

I spot a station and pull in swiftly. Tena jumps out and runs for the bathroom. "Hey is she alright" states of country swaging truck driver.

"She's fine, just must of ate something bad" I mutter, while moans rise from the bathroom.

Must fit in. Just frown and look away. If you smile you're a dead giveaway for being " a problem" as they say. And no matter how messy things got you couldn't wipe that stinking acid grin off your face for anything. Just the nature of the drug. Even if you weren't happy something inside of you was very, very happy. Tena emerges from the bathroom looking haggard.

"I just shit out the world, we have to figure a way to put it everything back together again" she whimpers.

" We destroyed the whole world and we have to put it back together again, you have to figure out a way to put it back together, we destroyed it, its all our faults, please put it back together" rapidly over and over.

"You drive and I will think about how to make it right" sliding on my black sunglasses. I am already sucked into the world Tena. If we destroyed the earth we can figure it out. we are just the people to get the job done. it's the least we can do.

Chapter 10

No Escape

If we did destroy the earth what could we do. I have know idea how to make it right. How to fix the planet after a destruction. Where would we start. How would we live. We could use our minds to overcome anything. Anything. Even a world totally destroyed by two acid tripping maniacs hell bent on finding the truth. If there is such a fantastical thing. I can see civilization. We must be in time to let the world know what's coming. We are on a very important mission to let them know their destruction is coming. They must know we have been sent by the highest authority to speak of things that will come to pass if we do not take another course of action.

I pull out the pipe and grab the stinky skunk we have had stashed on us the whole night. I figure if we were going to figure out this apocalypse mess we would need some green smoke. I puff the glorious skunk feeling the acid begin to rush back into my mind. I pass the pipe to Tena, thinking how we must hurry and get to town. They are throwing a rave and they must know what has happened. The world will be destroyed and we must warn everyone. If feels like the universe is riding shotgun on this journey and we are destined to be the messenger of the aliens. They are warning us through psychedelic hallucinatory realities of what will happen to our planet. They are here to warn us, not take over. Why cant they see what is going on. Our children wont have a world they would want to live in. The holy smoke is filling the car as we head full on into another peak. There is a white SUV we are riding behind very closely and getting closer.

Tena is riding right on their bumper going 70 mph.

"Every time I get to far away from the car in front, the road disappears" Tena barks holding onto the steering wheel for dear life.

It must be God leading the way. Recreating the world as we drive to the rave that will save the planet. We can save the planet through dance. Through celebration. Through passion for life. For love. God is driving the SUV. Piling down the highway of love giving two of her soldiers a escort. The city is coming into view and we are flying behind God going to the party of all parties. I look to the right as we pass 5 police cruisers with their lights on. They must be part of the escort to. We must be close. We better hurry before its all to late.

"What should I do?" exclaims Tena. "Hit it".

Tena slams on the gas as we sweep past the lit up cruisers. This is huge. The world must be coming to an end. That's a lot of cops. Tena is flying down the freeway and hit's the first off ramp going into downtown. Cops swarm from every direction. The world is now crumbling into pieces. Lights flash every where as Tena glides through the streets with ease. She rips down a main road leading into the center of downtown. The music in the car seems like it is coming from the sky. We are on a mission and everyone knows it. Tena takes a sharp left guided by our escorts blocking off the road as she slips right pass at high speed. Out of nowhere a cruiser flies up to our side containing a officer screaming like a mad man. Why is he so upset. We were led here by god to a party that will save the planet. Haven't you been notified. I guess this individual had not been because he was now in the process of trying to run of us off the road. Tena jumps the curb onto the sidewalk to go around and just as she pulls up on the sidewalk a woman and her child come walking out of a store. Tena yanks the car back onto the road and rams right into the side of the on coming cruiser. The metal shards blast off in slow motion as the cops crazed face falls off into the distance. This is it. We are about to cross over. Death is upon us. The road ahead is blocked, so Tena takes the only turn she can.

"What should I do, there's no where to go" Tena screams with sheer panic.

"Take it off the bridge, Ill take off my seatbelt" snapping off the belt from my side.

"What? No we are not, we are not dying today" jerking us into a parking lot on the side.

As soon as we pulled in we were surrounded by cruisers. Dozens of them. One cop jumped onto the roof of the car with a handgun and put the steel to the glass. I looked to my side and another cop was already bashing in Tena's face while she was still strapped into the seatbelt. I jumped out of the car to give chase and was struck in the back of the head with what I supposed to be a club of some sort. I could hear Tena screaming

"Why ,why, why are you doing this, they are here to help us the aliens are here to help us".

I was also screaming at the top my lungs as well. "I didn't do anything why are you doing this whhhhyyyyyyy".

The depths of depravity you can reach under these certain kinds of stress is horrible to say the least. The boots stomped my face from all sides. Cans of mace were sprayed in the ground and my face was rubbed into the puddles. It felt like my face was being melted off with a sand blaster. The boots and the clubs. Pounding from all sides. I was cuffed now and my feet tied together. A cord was run through the handcuffs and through my foot tie. Then they picked me up by the cord and folded my body backwards. It felt as if my guts had fallen out of my body and my spine snapped in half.

The kind officer then slammed me face first into the hood of his car. "Its all for world peace" he laughed pounding my face on his hood one more time for good measure.

They pushed me into the back of a cruiser. My face was on fire. Burning, burning, burning. Broadcasts were coming across the cruisers radio.

"mobs are throwing rocks at state house" "Riots in the streets" "Back up needed"

What the fuck was going on. Has the revolution started. Is it here. Did we cross into another dimension again? Keep your mouth shut. Don't say anything to them no matter what. Keep your mouth shut.

We were moving now as the broadcasts kept coming in over the radio. It didn't seem to phase the two officers one bit. Why would it. Its us against them right. They would never understand an alien race here to help us anyway. They would just want to shoot it, capture it, cut it up, and probably want to eventually eat it for dinner. The cops stop the car and a white gurney pulls up. it's a hospital and looks like I'm going to get checked out before they send me into the slammer. They handcuff me and strap down my feet to the gurney, just in case I lose it again I guess. I can already hear Tena screaming before we get into the ER.

"The mother ship is here to save us" "They are our friends" " They are trying to help us"

She screams it out over and over. They slide my gurney right beside her. She is screaming hysterically.

"Don't you fucking talk or Ill split you up, don't say a fucking word to each other." exclaims an invisible cop from somewhere around me.

The doctor presides to cut off Tena's clothes in front of the whole gang of police. They are having a great time.

"Maybe we should play some Pink Floyd for her" giggles one of the gang.

I cant see anything from the mace. I mean not a fucking thing. My eyes were swollen totally shut so forget getting a good look at these fine individuals. So I am handcuffed next to Tena while a group of cops is watching her get her clothes cut off by a doctor. Tena screams louder and louder. Now the screams are of pain and fear. One final blood curling scream. They just jammed a tube between her legs to get a urine sample to prove what she was on. Now she is silent. Just whimpers and sobs of tears. I am now trying to swallow my tongue. I have always heard of this method of suicide. You swallow your tongue and choke yourself to death. Its much, much harder to do than you think. The body has a hard time listening to the brain to do itself in. The nurse comes up to my side.

"It will be ok, just calm down and do what they say, it will be over real soon" her voice sounds like it was delivered from heaven itself.

Someone that cared. A warm feeling in the grasp of the pits.

"Go use the bathroom in this cup or they will get it another way just listen to them"

I don't know if this voice was coming from a person or from inside my head. I couldn't see anything and was still tripping my face off. They handcuffed me to the bathroom stall and I relived myself for their toxic records.

Good luck finding anything but that fine skunk. Acid needs the spine to be tapped to find it. I'm hoping that is not an option at this point. I don't hear anything from Tena anymore. They must have gave her the Thorazine. They give it to people who have psychotic breakdowns ,specifically for acid victims. It takes you right back to baseline in like ten seconds. Real quick. Slams the person back into their serotonin realities. Very dangerous and a very hard way to come down off acid. That's why you say nothing. Even if you see the alien mother ship overhead you just keep your mouth shut. Or in comes the treatment for the "sick" person. Granted we pushed the limits this time for sure.

I get shoved into a police van and away we go to the county jail. The acid is still searing in my mind. The walls of the van swish with black and gray mud that flows with the sway of the road. My clothes are torn to shreds and my face is still melting away from the mace. The grains of mace laced asphalt fill my face. The van stops and I hear the cops coming for the door.

I have lost all control over my salivary glands from the mace so I am slobbering everywhere.

"pull it together asshole your fucking up my van" expresses one of the fine drivers.

I slobber even more. Fuck these mother fuckers. They just rapped my girlfriend while she was handcuffed next to me and laughed like it was a fucking carnival. I am going to make a mess all the fucking way. What the fuck do I have to lose. They already beat the shit out of me what the fuck else could they do. I let the spit fly son. All over the fucking joint. I still couldn't see a dam thing. "Put your fingers up here for printing" a cold voice said as a felt someone grabbing my hands.

"Ugggghhh......" I spit out mucus and spit all over the desk. Good luck with those prints assholes.

"Get him out of here, we will get them on exit" shoves the voice from inside the invisible cage.

I get shoved into another room, which I think they call the drunk tank. I can see out of one of my eyes finally and its just a little room with a steel bed and toilet. The walls are still waving and moving in every direction. The ceiling looks like glass but I know its not. I don't believe anything I see anymore. How can I trust anything I think or do. I'm out of my mind. In every since of the word. The door opens and another person is shoved into the room. He is older than me and looks like he had a worse night than I did, if that's possible right? His arms are bandaged around his wrists and blood is dripping from them.

"I was tripping too man". "I didn't want to live anymore, so I just sliced them man" holding up his wounds proudly. He had made the cuts right through the throats of two dragons he had tattooed on his forearms. The dragons became alive and began slithering up and down the man's arms.

"Come on we are moving you to general, get moving" barks a guard from our cell door.

I swiftly leave the bleeding man, who gives a wicked smile. Was he real or not. I will never know.

I am handed my blues and slippers and told to change. The slippers are 4 sizes to small so my feet hang out onto the ground. The clothes are pretty much the same way. Small and sterile. They hand me my pillow and lead me toward the cells. The walls fold down around me and I can feel the evil lying here in this place. Pain, suffering, torment. Screams and sinister giggles. Demons rule here in this place. Maybe I should have got that Thorazine. Because this is not a place to be on acid in anyway shape or form. They lead me to the cell block door. There is no escape.

Chapter 11

Satan's Song

I entered the cell block in total darkness. The first thing
that hit you was the smell. The county lock up was built
next to the city dump. All the sewage that was processed
for the whole city passed just feet from the jail walls. The
smell was of dead human feces piled up on top of rotted
flesh. It was unbearably. The walls seeped of the foul
scent. Everything reeked of death. It was lights out so
most of the inmates were already bunked down. There
were Tv's in each corner that illuminated just fragments
of the surroundings. People lay strewn in every direction
with floor mats covering every inch of the floor. I looked
up at the ceiling of the prison and was astonished by the
sight.

The ceiling area had dissolved and I could see dozens of
alien figures peering into the cell block from above. It
seemed like they were observing something they had
never been able to access before. To look into the human
condition through the eyes of its caged animals. They
whispered and chatted vigorously among the council. I
looked for an empty spot on the floor and sat down with
my back on the wall. I had known enough people who
had gone to jail to know the basic rules of engagement.
Never leave your back exposed. No one is your friend. If
someone confronts you don't back down until the guards
stop it. No matter what. As I sat there watching the alien
council observe the humans, a tall black figure
approached from the darkness. It looked like a very large
shadow indeed. Like a 6' 7" 400 lb size shadow. It slowly
sits down right next to me and begins to speak.

"Will you be my friend" slips the massive shadow. "Not really looking for friends at this moment, just trying to get out of here" I shoot back sternly.

"Please be my friend. We can hang out, when we get out. I have no family and no one else in this world. We can be friends."

The shadow is now moving closer into my visual field. The TV lit up the creature just enough for me to get a good eye full. This shadow was a huge black man with empty, hollowed eyes. One of his arms was totally disfigured from what looked like a huge fire of some sort. The acid was making the wound come to life right in front of my eyes. I could see the fire melting his skin.

"Listen man, I have enough going on right now, I'm sorry I don't need any friends right now" I pushed while trying to position myself out of ear shot of melting man.

"Just chill on em smiley, this boy had enough today. You the white boy that rammed that cop right? vexed a voice from the darkness.

" You laced them suckers up good, what the fuck were you on?" "Acid, a lot of acid" I reply.

"Ohh that acid shit is crazy stuff, you out of your mind crazy white boy" giggled the voice from the abyss.

Now laughs were coming from all over the place. I thought I was alone but I was surrounded. The voice from the darkness now stepped forward. He was a tall, thin, muscular black man that obviously had much respect from the cellies around him. Smiley had backed off as soon as he spoke. I thought that was going to be the beginning of the end. He had three bigger guys sitting around him at a steel table. My eyes were adjusting to the darkness because I was making out more details of my surroundings.

"I'm L, L Furious homeboy and what's your name"

"Jay" I shyly reply seeing how the advantage was definitely in L's favor.

" I bet you would like some music being as fucked up as you are right? I could be the worlds greatest rapper if I could just stop selling crack" busting into hysterically laughter. The crew lit up with roaring laughter.

"Stop selling crack, you get it son, if I could just stop selling crack" slapping his knee at his own amusing joke.

One of his crew sitting at the table began banging on the steel table. Boom, pat, boom, boom, pat, boom ,pat, boom, boom, boom as L breaks off into satanic verse. He starts to speak of growing up in the scourges of the American nightmare. He rhythmically sweeps through tales of murder, corruption, loss, no hope. I could see the lost souls dammed to an eternity of slavery bound by their bloodline. Circumstantial witnesses to the ever growing pile of wasted human potential. As he spoke horns began to grow from his forehead and his legs bent backwards at the knees. Hoofs appeared where feet would be. His chin elongated, creasing to a sharp point.

L had just turned into the lord of darkness right in front of my face.

"Now you see the truth, the real truth. There is no hope. Ha ha a hah hahahahah!!!! Gleamed Mr. Furious.

The alien inspectors chattered louder than before, very, very excited by Mr. Furious speech. They seemed to have the information they had come for. Information from the Dark lord himself speaking through one of his darkest disciples. This was the voice of the dammed. A creature that gave up its soul long ago for the power that evil had offered up. Lost from birth, bound to streets of death to peddle the same fear to the next generation.

Not ever knowing any different. Someone ruffled in the darkness of the cell block. Another huge figure rises from the dark.

"Shut the fuck up, its late you've had your fun" gruffed the looming shadow.

Whoever this was meant business. The band of demons dispersed into the cracks darkness with the command. The sun was beginning to peer in through the frosted barred windows. Only a few more hours to see the judge. Hopefully Ill make bail. Get out of this god forsaken hell hole. I don't know what will happen to Tena. She was really out of if and I don't know if she will end up here at county or in the criminal mental hospital. I hope she finally calmed down. If you end up in the mental ward, you can end up there forever. They release you when they deem you are fit to return into society. I pray she didn't end up there. Complete exhaustion is setting in. My eyes are so heavy. Must stay awake. Never know what's going to happen in here. Keep guard up. Keep eyes open. Sooo tired.....

I drift off into a semi lucid dream state. I see Tena's beautiful face. I feel her touch on my skin. The warmth of her love showering over me. I miss her so much already.

We have become one. It feels like my arm has been cut off. I see her clear as day and grab for her. The world breaks into glass.

"Eh, eh you get up breakfast is coming eh wake up"

It was Smiley. He was shoving me to alert me breakfast was coming. I must have only slept an hour or so. The sun was gone but the rain was visible so it must be daytime. The door to the cellblock opened and a guard appeared. He had trays of food and another guard with him. Everyone lined up on the wall. I followed suit getting toward the back, not even waiting to think about eating any food whatsoever. I had mace and acid for lunch yesterday. Not feeling to hungry at this point. I grabbed the tray and sat down on the floor in my "space". A mat against the wall. My space. I sat down and just stared at the food. It was a cereal of some sort with hard bread and grapefruit juice. I down the juice and leave the rest. I'll throw up that shit for sure.

"Umm you want that jay, Ill take it from you" Smiley shyly quips.

I can now make out Smiley fully. He is huge, I was dead on about that. His arm was horribly deformed. But he wasn't scary at all. It seemed to me that he actual had some type of brain damage. He was very shy and had the mind of a child.

"You can take all of it Smiley, knock yourself out" handing over the tray.

"Oh thank you so much thank you thank you"

Well now I've got a friend for at least the duration of being in this block. We have a few minutes before we are bussed over to the court house to see the judge. Some of us are going, a lot of us are staying. Some of us are just waiting to go up to the higher prisons. Most caught up in the wrong place at the wrong time. Petty theft, dope dealers, scam artists, pimps, boyfriends on the wrong end of a bad fight, crack heads, alcoholics, homeless scavengers, redneck trailer park mutants. Wrong place wrong time type folks.

The lucky ones pile out into the hallway. Single file, one by one getting cuffed together as we emerge from the block. No one is allowed to speak now.

No talk on the bus, no talk in the halls. Just the guards barking to keep in line. Walk the fucking line on the floor. And believe it or not a lot of us didn't even know how to follow that basic instruction. Every now and then you'd hear the quick:

"Fuck you pig" "Fuck you mother fucker"

And this would usually follow with a little scuffling sound of boots, a few more last gasps of hate then back to silence again. I was cuffed to Smiley. He was so dam big they had to double cuff him. We hardly fit into the seat on the bus. The buses were big tourist type monsters with foreboding blackened windows. And again with the smell. A smell so pungent the body reels to not breathe. Just enough air through the lungs to stay alive. but the smell would get inside you. Rot. Human filthy rot. I really hope someone is here to bail my ass out. Please God get me out of this dam mess. The guards are passing out sandwiches before we get off the bus to go into the courtroom. Rotted sandwich meat on stale bread. How do these guys get so big in here eating this shit everyday. I cant even force myself to eat half. I hand the rest over to Smiley, who gorges down the rest with grumbling glee. Good ole Smiley. Now I know how he got his name. He never stops smiling. Ignorance is bliss as they say. And for Smiley it was a way of life.

The buses pull up to the gigantic concrete fortress known as the courthouse. It's a huge black structure. 40 floors or more of punishment. A huge beeping steel door raises as the bus pulls under the building. We enter into a tunnel that runs below the courthouse lined with guards and gun ports. They file us out two by two until the bus is empty. Another huge steel door beeps open and we are filed into another chamber. They break us into smaller groups. Each smaller group is put into an elevator. We ride up to an undisclosed floor and pile into a room the size of a walk-in closet. Our group consisted of at least 20 grown men stuffed into this steel box. This is where we would wait to see the judge. The smell. The fucking smell. Tension begins rising every second we are stuffed into the room. There is no air conditioning so every second it heats up another 10 degrees. People shove and sway to try and stay out of each others space. Looks get harder and voices get louder. The walls close in and the air is sucked out of the box. How fucking long. I'm losing my mind. I'm losing my mind. I'm losing my mind.

"Hudard, Your up" grunts a guard from behind the steel laced cage wall.

Thank god. Anything to get me the fuck out of here. Anything.

I entered the courtroom for the most humiliating scene I

would ever have to go through. The whole courtroom is filled with my family. My mom, my brother, my aunts and uncles, everyone came down for the show. You want to talk about embarrassing. The waves of fear were long gone compared to the bottomless feeling of total failure. Being marched in front of my family for display. A animal run astray that needed brought before the town for his punishment. Look at what your son has become. A bitter, bitter taste indeed. I could read their minds clear as day:

"Where did I do wrong" "You fucking idiot you did it this time" "What the fuck were you thinking" "Oh god I hope this doesn't happen to my kids" "Where did I go wrong" "Where did I go wrong"

My poor mom's tear soaked face. She had been put through it. Her and my dad both. I'm sure they are happy I'm still alive. I don't know how I am to tell you the truth. I stood before the judge as they discussed my bail. They were charging me with resisting arrest, dis- orderly conduct, evading the police, and assault on a police officer. Holy crap. It didn't sound good at all. They beat the shit out me and my only hope for reduction was taking pictures before the wounds healed. Please let the bail ride. This was my first offense so the judge showed mercy on the fucked up idiot. Bail was set for 5,000. That meant I would have to cover 500. Oh please let my parents have it.

We are so poor. I don't know if they will but I am sure hoping. Im praying with every cell in my body that they have the power to get me the fuck out of here. I will be a good boy, I promise. Play the straight game. Play by the rules. The guard ushered me out of the courtroom and back to the human sweat shack. I'll know in a few hours if I am getting out of this place. May the gods have mercy on my sweet soul.

Chapter 12

Hopeless Reunion

The bus trip back to the county lock up was longer this time. Only questions float through my mind. Am I going to get out of here? Are my parents going to bail me? What happened to Tena? The questions swim in the rain pouring down on the bus. The world looks dead. Gray with pain. A shadow world of the bright world I once knew. A world of creativity and friendships replaced with suffering and doubt. Paranoia and confusing. I notice Smiley isn't on the bus. He must have got released on site. Good ole Smiley, I knew the guy for less than 24 hours but I will never forget him. We are placed back into our cells in the usual fashion. I was totally sober now and reality was closing in on me fast. The looks were now harder. New inmates were coming in. Pissed, ready to fight. Ready for anything to take away the pain. For just a moment. Even if it meant causing someone else pain.

I found my place back on my wall and flopped down my ravaged body. My whole body ached from head to toe. My hair was falling out by the fist full from the cops makeover. Inmates were playing cards. Yelling at each other in a language invented in their neighborhoods. Gang signs were thrown to let people know where that neighborhood was located. Neighborhoods stayed together. Races stayed together. The most basic of human traits. Territorially pissing on the walls of the man. They didn't even know they were created by the same system that they fight so hard against. To rebel right into the arms of a master centuries old. I closed my eyes, trying to climb out of this abyss. Try and hold on to why I want to live. Why I want to love. Why I want to try for a better world. Mostly running over images of Tena. Over and over. Her face, her eyes, her laugh. I realize now more than anytime before that I love her. No matter what we have been through. No matter what we have done. I love her beyond the limits of our boundless universe. I don't want to die. I want life. I want a life with her. As the saying goes: "You don't know what you have until you get into a high speed police chase and destroy your life."

The hours passed into a murky hell. It seemed like days waiting to hear something. Anything. And finally it came down from above.

"Hudard, your out here" trumpeted the guard.

Oh let sweet freedom ring. Gotta keep cool. Still have time in here. Dudes would love to fuck up someone getting released. You can feel that hate and jealously like a blanket.

"Fucking white boy, out in a day I'd get 10 years for that shit" pipes an old black man who looked like he had been here 20 years already.

Fuck. Just play it cool. Ignore it. Be cool. Your almost free. Just be cool. The cellblock door finally opens.

"Hudard, Mckenna, Leary your out"

I jump up with angel wings and head for the door. They take me down to the release station. Its packed from wall to wall with inmates heading out. The mood in this section is very different. Homeboys hitting high fives, almost bouncing off the ground with happiness. Wide smiles with the sentence " FUCK YOU" written all over their faces. I get called up to the reception window and get released my artifacts. My ripped shirt and my cut up jeans. They cut my jeans off me at the hospital, so they were cut up to the crotch. I'm directed to the camera aisle for my head shot and tattoo assessment. "Turn to the right" "Turn to the left" "Face front" Now it was official.

I was a fully registered criminal of the state. I real menace to society. I was led down another bland hallway to a glass door with a reception window at it.

"Papers." guided the clerk I handed them over and she stamped them clean. "Open the gate, release prisoner" The glass door opens and the bird is free baby. Fucking free.

I step out into the cool night breeze. The rain is coming down in sheets. No one is there. I don't know who is coming for me. I'm guessing its my parents. Has to be. I don't know anyone else that would bail me out. I wonder where Tena is. A crushing feeling of despair wraps around my heart. Where is she? Did she already get out? Her parents are never going to let me see her again. I've lost her. For good. I've lost her. Oh god please no. I start to panic. That sweet feeling of freedom is now transformed into utter panic. What will I do without her? What if she isn't ok? What if she isn't getting out? I begin running up and down the barbed wire fence surrounding the prison. I run frantically from side to side peering into the muck looking for any sign of hope. I'm crying like a lunatic at this point. Screaming Tena's name into the drowning sky. I'm waving my arms around trying to get inmates attention. Maybe they know her. Maybe they will tell her to look outside. I need to let her know I love her.

That I will wait for her.

I lean against the fence in total defeat. This is hopeless. If she is in there I will never know. She wont see me. I need to let go. I clinch my fists around the fence. The pain is to much. The pain of it all. The pain of life. The pain of this world. Pain down to the very core of my mortal soul. The tears are falling harder than the rain now. Rivers of pain being released from my body. I will see her again.

I know it. I can feel her in my bones. She is ok. I know it. I can feel hope drip back into my body. The tears are slowing and my spirit is rising. I notice the release doors open. Light breaks through on a little shadow of a figure. Is it her. Cant tell yet. Is it her. I fight the feeling of running up to the unknown figure. It could be anyone. Anyone indeed.

"Jay?" whispers a voice from the darkness. "Tena, is that you?

And before we could answer, we had already fallen into each others arms. We held each other so tight the wind was drawn from both our lungs. No words just tears. The rain poured down onto us with a blessing from the sky. We were one. Together again. and we made it together. We had been through it folks. Down the tunnel into a world of free wheeling madness and mayhem. We had pushed the limits of this world that's for sure. We had discovered brand new vistas within the human mind never before witnessed. Landed in strange new worlds. Worlds we hadn't even known existed before we opened up the Pandora's box of the human mind. Where would we go from here only the stars would know. But one thing is for sure.

We had seen the Other Side of This.

For more information on this book or its author please contact the following:

othersideofthisbook@gmail.com

jeffhubb09@gmail.com
or
(USA)1-323-804-2624